MASTERS OF EVOLUTION

Damon Knight

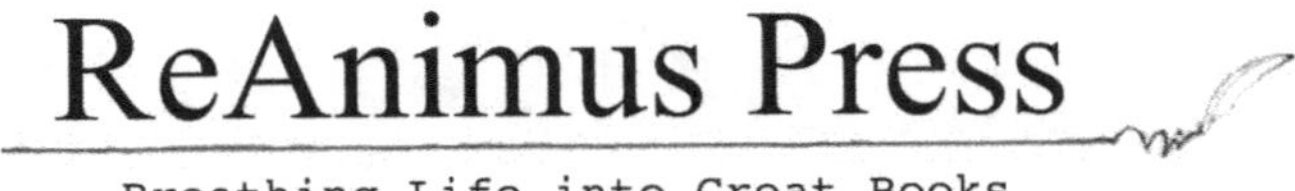

ReAnimus Press

Breathing Life into Great Books

ReAnimus Press
1100 Johnson Road #16-143
Golden, CO 80402
www.ReAnimus.com

ISBN-13: 9798590210480

First ReAnimus Press print edition: January, 2021

2101031703
10 9 8 7 6 5 4 3 2 1

I

The most promising young realie actor in Greater New York, everyone agreed, was a beetle-browed Apollo named Alvah Gustad. His diction, which still held overtones of the Under Flushing labor pool, the unstudied animal grace of his movements and his habitually sullen expression enabled him to dominate any stage not occupied by an unclothed woman at least as large as himself. At twenty-six, he had a very respectable following among the housewives of Manhattan, Queens, Jersey and the rest of the seven boroughs. The percentage of blown fuses resulting from subscribers' attempts to clutch his realized image was extraordinarily low — Alvah, his press agents explained with perfect accuracy, left them too numb.

Young Gustad, who frequently made his first entrance water-beaded as from the shower, with a towel girded chastely around his loins, was nevertheless in his private life a modest and slightly bewildered citizen, much given to solitary reading, and equipped with a perfect set of the conventional virtues.

These included cheerful performance of all municipal duties and obligations — like every right-thinking citizen, Gustad held down two jobs in summer and three in winter. At the moment, for example, he was an actor by day and a metals-reclamation supervisor by night.

Chief among his less tangible attributes, was that emotion which in some ages has been variously described as civic pride or patriotism. In A.D. 2064, as in B.C. 400, they amounted to the same thing.

Behind the Manager's desk, the wall was a single huge slab of black duroplast, with a map of the city picked out in pinpoints of brilliance. As Gustad entered with his manager and his porter, an unseen chorus of basso profundos broke into the strains of *The Slidewalks of New York*. After four bars, it segued to *New York, New York, It's a Pip of a Town* and slowly faded out.

The Manager himself, the Hon. Boleslaw Wytak, broke the reverent hush by coming forward to take Alvah's hand and lead him toward the desk. "Mr. Gustad—and Mr. Diamond, isn't it? Great pleasure to have you here. I don't know if you've met all these gentlemen. Commissioner Laurence, of the Department of Extramural Relations—Director Ostertag, of the Bureau of Vital Statistics—Chairman Neddo, of the Research and Development Board."

Wytak waited until everyone was comfortably settled in one of the reclining chairs which fitted into slots in the desk, with cigars, cigarettes, liquor capsules and cold snacks at each man's elbow. "Now, Mr. Gustad—and Mr. Diamond—I'm a plain blunt man and I know you're wondering why I asked you to come here today. I'm going to tell you. The City needs a man with great talent and great courage to do a job that, I tell you frankly, I wouldn't undertake myself without great misgivings." He gazed at Gustad warmly, affectionately but sternly. "You're the man, Alvah."

Little Jack Diamond cleared his throat nervously. "What kind of a job did you have in mind, Mr. Manager? Of course, anything we can do for our city..."

Wytak's big face, without perceptibly moving a muscle, somehow achieved a total change of expression. "Alvah, I want you to go to the Sticks."

Gustad blinked and tilted upright in his chair. He looked at Diamond.

The little man suddenly seemed two sizes smaller inside his box-cut cloth-of-silver tunic. He gestured feebly and wheezed, *"Wake-me-up!"* The porter behind his chair stepped forward alertly, clanking, and flipped open one of the dozens of metal and plastic boxes that clung to him all over like barnacles. He popped a tiny capsule into his palm, rolled it expertly to thumb-and-finger position, broke it under Diamond's nose.

A reeking-sweet green fluid dripped from it and ran stickily down the front of Diamond's tunic.

"Dumbhead!" said Diamond. "Not cream de menthy, a wake-me-up!" He sat up as the abashed servant produced another capsule. "Never mind." Some color was beginning to come back into his face. *"Blotter!"* A wad of absorbent fibers. *"Vacuum!"* A lemon-sized globe with a flaring snout. *"Gon-Stink! Presser!"*

Gustad looked back at the Manager. "Your Honor, you mean you want me to go into the Sticks? I mean," he said, groping for words, "you want me to play for the *Muckfeet?"*

"That is just exactly what I want you to do." Wytak nodded toward the Commissioner, the Director, and the Chairman. "These gentlemen are here to tell you why. Suppose you start, Ozzie."

Ostertag, the one with the fringe of yellowish white hair around his potato-colored pate, shifted heavily and stared at Gustad. "In my bureau, we have records of population and population density, imports and exports, ratio of births to deaths and so on that go back all the way to the time of the United States. Now this isn't known generally, Mr. Gustad, but although New York has been steadily growing ever since its founding in 1646, our growth in the last thirty years has been entirely due to immigration from other less fortunate cities.

"In a way, it's fortunate—I mean to say that we can't expand *horizontally*, because it has been found impossible to eradicate the soil organisms—" a delicate shudder ran around the group—"left by our late enemies. And as for continuing to build vertically— well, since Pittsburgh fell, we have been dependent almost entirely on salvaged scrap for our steel. To put it bluntly, unless something is done about this situation, the end is in sight. Not alone of this administration, but of the city as well. Now the *reasons* for this—ah—what shall I say..."

With his head back, staring at the ceiling, Wytak began to speak so quietly that Ostertag blundered through another phrase and a half before he realized he had been interrupted.

"Thirty years ago, when I first came to this town, an immigrant kid with nothing in the whole world but the tunic on my back and the gleam in my eye, we had just got through with the last of the Muckfeet Wars. According to your history books, we won that war. I'll tell you something—we were licked!"

Alvah squirmed uncomfortably as Wytak raised his head and glanced defiantly around the desk, looking for contradiction. The Manager said, "We drove them back to the Ohio, thirty years ago. And where are they now?" He turned to Laurence. "Phil?"

Laurence rubbed his long nose with a bloodless forefinger. "Their closest settlement is twelve miles away. That's to the southwest, of course. In the west and north—"

"Twelve miles," said Wytak reflectively. "But that isn't the reason I say they licked us. They licked us because there are twenty million of us today... and about one hundred fifty million of them. Right, Phil?"

Laurence said, "Well, there aren't any accurate figures, you know, Boley. There hasn't been any census of the Muckfeet for almost a century, but—"

"About one hundred fifty million," interrupted Wytak. "Even if we formed a league with every other city on this continent, the odds would be heavily against us—and they breed like flies." He slapped the desk with his open palm. "So do their filthy animals!"

A shudder rippled across the group. Diamond shut his eyes tight.

"There it is," said Wytak. "Rome fell. Babylon fell. The same thing can happen to New York. Those illiterate savages will go on increasing year by year, getting more ignorant and more degraded with every generation... and a century from now — or two, or five — *they'll be the human race.* And New York..."

Wytak turned to look at the map behind him. His hand touched a button and the myriad tiny lights went out.

Gustad was not an actor who wept readily, but he felt tears welling over his eyelids. At the same time, the thought crossed his mind that, competition being what it was in the realies, it was a good thing that Wytak had gone into politics instead of acting.

"Sir," he said, "what can we do?"

Wytak's eyes were focused far away. After a moment, his head turned heavily on his massive shoulders, like a gun turret. "Chairman Neddo has the answer to that. I want you to listen carefully to what he's going to tell you, Alvah."

Neddo's crowded small face flickered through a complicated series of twitches, all centripetal and rapidly executed. "Over the past several years," he said jerkily, "under Manager Wytak's direction, we have been developing certain devices, certain articles of commerce, which are designed, especially designed, to have an attraction for the Muckfeet. Trade articles. Most of these, I should say all—"

"Trade articles," Wytak cut in softly. "Thank you, Ned. That's the phrase that tells the story. Alvah, we're going to go back to the principles that made our ancestors great. Trade — expanding markets — expanding industries. Think about it. From the Arctic Ocean to the Gulf of Mexico, there are some 150 million people who haven't got a cigarette lighter or a wristphone or a realie set among them. Alvah, we're going to civilize the Muckfeet. We've put together a grab-bag of modern science, expressed in ways their primitive minds can understand — and *you're* the man who's going to sell it to them! What do you say to that?"

This was a familiar cue to Gustad — it had turned up for the fiftieth or sixtieth time in his last week's script, when he had played the role of a kill-crazy sewer inspector, trapped by flood waters in the cloacae of Under Brooklyn. "I say—" he began, then realized that his usual response was totally inappropriate. "It sounds wonderful," he finished weakly.

Wytak nodded in a businesslike way. "Now here's the program." He pressed a button, and a relief map of the North American continent appeared on the wall behind him. "Indicator." Wytak's porter put a metal tube with a shaped grip into his hand—a tiny spot on the map fluoresced where he pointed it.

"You'll swing down to the southwest until you cross the Tennessee, then head westward about to here, then up through the Plains, then back north of the Great Lakes and home again. You'll notice that this route keeps you well clear of both Chicago and Toronto. Remember that—it's important. We know that Frisco is working on a project similar to ours, although they're at least a year behind us. If we know that, the chances are that the other Cities know it too, but we're pretty sure there's been no leak in our own security. There isn't going to be any."

He handed the indicator back. "You'll be gone about three months..."

Diamond was having trouble with his breathing again.

"... You'll have to rough it pretty much—there'll be room in your floater for you and your equipment, and that's all."

Diamond gurgled despairingly and rolled up his eyes. Gustad himself felt an unpleasant sinking sensation.

"You mean," he asked incredulously, "I'm supposed to go all by myself—without even a *porter?*"

"That's right," said Wytak. "You see, Alvah, you and I are civilized human beings—we know there are so many indispensable time and labor saving devices that nobody could possibly carry them all himself. But could you explain that to a Muckfoot?"

"I guess not."

"That's why only a man with your superb talents can do this job for the City. Those people actually live the kind of sordid brutal existence you portray so well in the realies. Well, you can be as rough and tough as they are—you can talk their own language, and they'll respect you."

Gustad flexed his muscles slightly, feeling pleased but not altogether certain. Then a new and even more revolting aspect of this problem occurred to him. "Your Honor, suppose I got along *too* well with the Muckfeet? I mean suppose they invited me into one of their houses to—" he gagged slightly—"eat?"

Wytak's face went stony. "I am surprised that you feel it necessary to bring that subject up. All that will be covered very thoroughly in the briefing you will get from Commissioner Laurence and Chairman Neddo and their staffs. And I want you to understand, Gustad, that no pressure of any kind is being exerted on you to take this assignment. This is a job for a willing, cooperative volunteer, not a draftee. If you feel you're not the man for it, just say so now."

Gustad apologized profusely. Wytak interrupted him, with the warmest and friendliest smile imaginable. "That's all right, son, I understand. I understand perfectly. Well, gentlemen, I think that's all."

As soon as they were alone, Diamond clutched Gustad's sleeve and pulled him over to the side of the corridor. "Listen to me, Al boy. We can still pull you out of this. I know a doctor that will make you so sick you couldn't walk across the street. He wouldn't do it for everybody, but he owes me a couple of—"

"No, wait a minute. I don't—"

"I know, I *know*," said Diamond impatiently. "You'll get your contract busted with Seven Boroughs and you'll lose a couple months, maybe more, and you'll have to start all over again with one of the little studios, but what of it? In a year or two, you'll be as good as—"

"Now, wait, Jack. In the first—"

"Al, I'm not just thinking about my twenty per cent of you. I don't even *care* about that—it's just money. What I want, I want you should still be alive next year, you understand what I mean?"

"Look," said Gustad, "you don't understand, Jack. I *want* to go. I mean I don't exactly want to, but—" He pointed down the corridor to the window that framed a vista of gigantic columns, fiercely brilliant below, fading to massive darkness above, with a million tiny floater-lights drifting like a river of stardust down the avenue. "Just look at that. It took thousands of years to build! I mean if I can keep it going just by spending three months...

"And besides," he added practically, "think of the publicity."

II

The foothill country turned out to be picturesque but not very rewarding. Alvah had by-passed the ancient states of Pennsylvania and Maryland as directed, since the tribes nearest the city were understood to be still somewhat rancorous. By the end of his first day, he was beginning to regard this as a serious understatement.

He had brought his floater down, with flags flying, loudspeakers blaring, colored lights flashing and streamers flapping gaily behind him, just outside an untidy collection of two-story beehive huts well south of the former Pennsylvania border. He had seen numerous vaguely human shapes from the air, but when he extruded his platform and stepped out, every visible door was shut, the streets were empty, and there was no moving thing in sight, except for a group of singularly unpleasant-looking animals in a field to his right.

After a few moments, Gustad shut off the loudspeakers and listened. He thought he heard a hum of voices from the nearest building. Suppressing a momentary qualm, he lowered himself on the platform stair and walked over to the building. It had a single high window, a crude oval in shape, closed by a discolored pane.

Standing under this window, Alvah called, "Hello in there!"

The muffled voices died away for a moment, then buzzed as busily as ever.

"Come on out — I want to talk to you!"

Same result.

"You don't have to be afraid! I come in peace!"

The voices died away again, and Alvah thought he saw a dim face momentarily through the pane. A single voice rose on an interrogative note.

"Peace!" Alvah shouted.

The window slid abruptly back into the wall and, as Alvah gaped upward, a deluge of slops descended on him, followed by a gale of coarse laughter.

Alvah's immediate reaction, after the first dazed and gasping instant, was a hot-water-and-soap tropism, carrying with it an ardent desire to get out of his drenched clothes and throw them away. His second, as imperious as the first, had the pure flame of artistic inspiration—he wanted to see how many esthetically satisfying small pieces one explosive charge would make out of that excrescence-shaped building.

Under no conditions, said the handbook he had been required to memorize, *will you commit any act which might be interpreted by the Muckfeet as aggressive, nor will you make use of your weapons at any time, unless such use becomes necessary for the preservation of your own life.*

Alvah wavered, grew chilly and retired. Restored in body, but shaken in spirit, he headed south.

Then there had been his encounter with the old man and the animal. Somewhere in the triangle of land between the Mississippi and the Big Black, at a point which was not on his itinerary at all, but had the overwhelming attraction of being more than a thousand air-miles from New York, he had set the floater down near another sprawling settlement.

As usual, all signs of activity in and around the village promptly disappeared. With newly acquired caution, Alvah sat tight. Normal human curiosity, he reasoned, would drive the Muckfeet to him sooner or later—and even if that failed, there was his nuisance value. How long could you ignore a strange object, a few hundred yards from your home, that was shouting, waving flags, flashing colored lights and sending up puffs of pink-and-green smoke?

Nothing happened for a little over an hour. Then, half dozing in his control chair, Alvah saw two figures coming toward him across the field.

Alvah's ego, which had been taking a beating all day, began to expand. He stepped out onto the platform and waited.

The two figures kept coming, taking their time. The tall one was a skinny loose-jointed oldster with a conical hat on the back of his head. The little one ambling along in front of him was some sort of four-footed animal.

In effect, an audience of one—at any rate, it was Alvah's best showing so far. He mentally rehearsed his opening lines. There was no point, he thought, in bothering with the magic tricks or the comic monologue. He might as well go straight into the sales talk.

The odd pair was now much closer, and Gustad recognized the animal half of it. It was a so-called watchdog, one of the incredibly destructive beasts the Muckfeet trained to do their fighting for them. It had a slender, supple body, a long feline tail and a head that looked something like a terrier's and something like a house-cat's. However, it was not half as large or as frightening in appearance as the pictures Alvah had seen. It must, he decided, be a pup.

Two yards from the platform, the oldster came to a halt. The watchdog sat down beside him, tongue lolling wetly. Alvah turned off the loudspeakers and the color displays.

"Friend," he began, "I'm here to show you things that will astound you, marvels that you wouldn't believe unless you saw them with your own—"

"You a Yazoo?"

Thrown off stride, Alvah gaped. "What was that, friend?"

"Ah *said*—you a Yazoo?"

"No," said Alvah, feeling reasonably positive.

"Any kin to a Yazoo?"

"I don't think so."

"Git," said the old man.

Unlikely as it seemed, a Yazoo was apparently a good thing to be. "Wait a second," said Alvah. "Did you say *Yazoo?* I didn't understand you there at first. Am I a *Yazoo!* Why, man, my whole family on both sides has been—" what was the plural of Yazoo?

"Ah'll count to two," said the old man. "*One.*"

"Now wait a minute," said Alvah, feeling his ears getting hot. The watchdog, he noticed, had hoisted its rump a fraction of an inch and was staring at him in a marked manner. He flexed his right forearm slightly and felt the reassuring pressure of the pistol in its pop-out holster. "What makes you Muckfeet think you can—"

"*Two,*" said the oldster, and the watchdog was a spread-eagled blur in midair, seven feet straight up from the ground.

Instinct took over. Instinct had nothing to do with pistols or holsters, or with the probable size of a full-grown Muckfoot watchdog. It launched Alvah's body into a backward standing broad jump through the open floater door, and followed that with an economical underhand punch at the control button inside.

The door slammed shut. It then bulged visibly inward and rang like a gong. Sprawled on the floor, Gustad stared at it incredulously. There were further sounds—a thunderous growling and a series of hackle-raising skreeks, as of hard metal being gouged by something even harder. The whole floater shook.

Alvah made the control chair in one leap, slammed on the power switch and yanked at the steering bar. At an altitude of about a hundred feet, he saw the dark shape of the watchdog leap clear and fall, twisting.

A few seconds later, he put the bar into neutral and looked down. Man and watchdog were moving slowly back across the field toward the settlement. As far as Alvah could tell, the beast was not even limping.

Alvah's orders were reasonably elastic, but he had already stretched them badly in covering the southward leg of his route in one day. Still, there seemed to be nothing else to do. Either there was an area somewhere on the circuit where he could get the

Muckfeet to listen to him, or there wasn't. If there was, it would make more sense to hop around until he found it, and then work outward to its limits, than to blunder straight along, collecting bruises and insults.

And if there wasn't—and this did not bear thinking about—then the whole trip was a bust.

Alvah switched on his communicator and tapped out the coded clicks that meant, "Proceeding on schedule"—which was a lie—"no results yet"—which was true. Then he headed north.

Nightfall overtook him as he was crossing the Ozark Plateau. He set the floater's controls to hover at a thousand feet, went to bed and slept badly until just before dawn. With a cup of kaffin in his hand, he watched this phenomenon in surprised disapproval: The scattered lights winking out below, the first colorless hint of radiance, which illuminated nothing, but simply made the Universe seem more senselessly vast and formless than before; finally, after an interminable progression of insignificant changes, the rinds of orange and scarlet, and the dim Sun bulging up at the rim of the turning Earth.

It was lousy theater.

How, Alvah asked himself, could any human being keep himself from dying of sheer irrelevance and boredom against a background like that? He was aware that billions had done so, but his general impression of history was that people who didn't have a city always got busy improving themselves until they could build one or take one away from somebody else. All but the Muckfeet...

Once their interest has been engaged, said the handbook at one point, *you will lay principal stress upon the competitive advantages of each product. It will be your aim to create a situation in which ownership of one or more of our products will be not only an economic advantage, but a mark of social distinction. In this way, communities which have accepted the innovations will, in order to preserve and extend the recognition of their own status, be forced to convert members of neighboring communities.*

Well, maybe so.

Alvah ate a Spartan breakfast of protein jelly and citron cakes, called in the coordinates and the time to the frog-voiced operator in New York, and headed the floater northward again.

The landscape unrolled itself. If there were any major differences between this country and the districts he had seen yesterday, Alvah was unable to discern them. In the air, he saw an occasional huge flapping shape, ridden by human figures. He avoided them, and they ignored him. Below, tracts of dark-green forest alternated predictably with the pale green, red or violet of cultivated fields. Here and there across the whole visible expanse, isolated buildings stood. At intervals, these huddled closer and closer together and became a settlement. There were perhaps more roads as he moved northward, dustier ones. That was all.

The dustiness of these roads, it occurred to Alvah, was a matter that required investigation. The day was cloudless and clear; there was no wind at Alvah's level, and nothing in the behavior of the trees or cultivated plants to suggest that there was any farther down.

He slowed the floater and lowered it toward the nearest road. As he approached, the thread of ocher resolved itself into an irregular series of expanding puffs, each preceded by a black dot, the overall effect being that of a line of black-and-tan exclamation points. They seemed to be moving just perceptibly, but were actually, Alvah guessed, traveling at a fairly respectable clip.

He transferred his attention to another road. It, too, was filled with hurrying dots, as was the next—and all the traffic was heading in approximately the same direction, westward of Alvah's course.

He swung the control bar over. The movement below, he was able to determine after twenty minutes' flying, converged upon a settlement larger than any he had yet seen. It sprawled for ten miles or more along the southern shore of a long and exceedingly narrow lake. Most of it looked normal enough—a haphazard arrangement of cone-roofed buildings — but on the side away from the lake, there was a fairly extensive area filled with what seemed to be long, narrow sheds. This, in turn, was bounded on two sides by a strip of fenced-in plots in which, as nearly as Alvah could make out through the dust, animals of all sizes and shapes were penned. It was this area which appeared to be the goal of every Muckfoot in the central Plains.

The din was tremendous as Alvah floated down. There were shouts, cries, animal bellowings, sounds of hammering, occasional blurts of something that might be intended to be music, explosions of laughter. The newcomers, he noted, were being herded with much confusion to one or another of the fenced areas, where they left their mounts. Afterward, they straggled across to join the sluggish river of bodies in the avenues between the sheds.

No one looked up or noticed the dim shadow of the floater. Everyone was preoccupied, shouting, elbowing, blowing an instrument, climbing a pole. Alvah found a clear space at some distance from the sheds — as far as he could conveniently get from the penned animals — and landed.

He had no idea what this gathering was about. For all he knew, it might be a war council or some kind of religious observance, in which case his presence might be distinctly unwelcome. But in any case, there were customers here.

He looked dubiously at the stud that controlled his attention-catchers. If he used them, he would only be following directives, but he had a strong feeling that it would be a faux pas. At the other extreme, the obvious thing to do was to get out and go look for someone in authority. This would involve abandoning the protection of the floater, however, and he might blunder into some taboo place or ceremony.

Evidently his proper course was to wait unobtrusively until he was discovered. On the other hand, if he stayed inside the floater with the door shut, the Muckfeet might take more alarm than if he showed himself. Still, wasn't it possible that they would be merely puzzled by a floater, whereas they would be angered by a floater with a man on its platform? Or, taking it from another angle...

The hell with it.

Alvah ran the platform out, opened the door and stepped out. He was relieved when, as he was considering the delicate problem of whether or not to lower the stair, a small group of men and urchins came into view around the corner of the nearest shed, a dozen yards away from him.

They stopped when they saw him, and two or three of the smallest children scuttled behind their elders. They exchanged looks and a few words that Alvah couldn't hear. Then a pudgy little man with a fussed expression crowded forward, and the rest followed him at a discreet distance.

"Hello," said Alvah tentatively.

The little man came to a halt a yard or so from the platform. He had a white badge of some kind pinned to his shapeless brown jacket, and carried a sheaf of papers in his hand. "Who might *you* be?" he asked irritably.

"Alvah Gustad is my name. I hope I'm not putting you people out, parking in your area like this, Mr.—"

"Well, I should hope to spit you *is*, though. Supposed to be a tent go up right *there*. Got to be one by noon. What did you say your name was, Gus what?"

"Gustad. I don't believe I caught your name, Mr.—"

"Don't signify what *my* name is. We talking about *you*. What clan you belong to?"

"Uh—Flatbush," said Alvah at random. "Look, as long as I'm in the way here, you just tell me where to move to and—"

"Some little backwoods clan, I never even *heard* of it," said the pudgy man. "*I'll* tell you where you can *move* to. You can just haul that thing back where you come from. Gustad—Flatbush! *You* ain't on my list, I know *that*."

The other Muckfeet had moved up gradually to surround the little man. One of them, a lanky sad-faced youngster, nudged him with his elbow. "Might just check and see, Jake."

"Well, I ought to know. My *land,* Artie, I got my *work* to do. *I* can't spend all day standing here."

Artie's long face grew more mournful. "You thought them Keokuks wasn't on the list, either."

"Well—all right then, rot it." To Alvah: "What's your marks?"

Alvah blinked. "I don't—"

"Come *down* offa there." Jake turned impatiently to a man behind him. "Give'm a stake." As Alvah came hesitantly down the stair, he found he was being offered a sharpened length of wood by a seamy-faced brown man, who carried a bundle of others like it under his arm.

Alvah took it, without the least idea of what to do next. The brown man watched him alertly. "You c'n make your marks with that," he volunteered and pointed to the ground between them.

The others closed in a little.

"Marks?" said Alvah worriedly.

The brown man hesitated, then took another stake from his bundle. "Like these here," he said. "These is mine." He drew a shaky circle and put a dot in the center of it. "George." A figure four. "Allister—that's me." A long rectangle with a loop at each end. "Coffin—that's m' clan."

Jake burst out, "Well, crying in a bucket, *he* knows that! You know how to sign your *name,* don't you?"

"Well," said Alvah, "yes." He wrote *Alvah Gustad* and, as an afterthought, added *Flatbush.*

There were surprised whistles. "Wrote it just as slick as Doc!" said a ten-year-old tow-headed male, bug-eyed with awe.

Jake stared at Alvah, then spun half around to wave his papers under Artie's nose. "Well, you satisfied now, Artie Brumbacher? I guess *that* ain't on my list, is it?"

"No," Artie admitted, "I guess it ain't—not if you can read the list, that is."

Everybody but Alvah laughed, Jake louder than anyone. "All right," he said, turning back to Alvah, "you just hitch up your brutes and get that thing *out* of here. If you ain't gone by the time I—"

"Jake!" called a businesslike female voice, and a small figure came shouldering through the crowd. "They need you over in the salamander shed—the Quincies is ready to move in, but there's some Sullivans ahead of them." She glanced at Alvah, then at the floater behind him. "You having any trouble here?"

"All settled *now*," Jake told her. "This feller ain't on the list. I just give him his *marching* orders."

"Look, if I can say something—" Alvah began.

The girl interrupted him. "Did you want to exhibit something at the Fair?"

"That's right," said Alvah gratefully. "I was just trying to explain—"

"Well, you late, but maybe we can squeeze you in. You won't sell anything, though, if it's what I think it is. Let me see that list, Jake."

"Now *wait* a minute," said Jake indignantly. "You know we ain't got room for nobody that ain't on the *list*. We got enough trouble—"

"The Earth-movers won't be here from Butler till tomorrow," said the girl, examining the papers. "We can put him in there and move him out again when they get here. You need any equipment besides what you brought?"

"No," said Alvah. "That would be fine, thanks. All I need is a place—"

"All right. Before you go, Jake, did you tell those Sullivans they could have red, green and yellow in the salamander shed?"

"Well, *sure* I did. That what it says right there."

She handed him back the papers and pointed to a line. "That Quincy, see? Dot instead of a cross. Sullivans is supposed to have that corner in the garden truck shed, keep the place warm for the seedlings, but they won't budge till you tell them it was a mistake. Babbishes and Stranahans is fit to be tied. You get over there and straighten them out, will you? And don't worry too much about *him*."

Jake snorted and moved away, still looking ruffled. The girl turned to Alvah. "All right, let's go."

Unhappy but game, Alvah turned and climbed back into the floater with the girl close behind him. The conditioning he'd had just before he left helped when he was in the open air, but in the tiny closed cabin of the floater the girl's triply compounded stench was overpowering.

How did they live with themselves?

She leaned over the control chair, pointing. "Over there," she said. "See that empty space I'm pointing at?"

Alvah saw it and put the floater there as fast as the generator would push it. The space was not quite empty—there were a few very oddly assorted Muckfeet and animals in it, but they straggled out when they saw him hovering, and he set the floater down.

To his immense relief, the girl got out immediately. Alvah followed her as far as the platform.

III

In the tailor shop back in Middle Queens, the proprietors, two brothers named Wynn, whose sole livelihood was the shop, stared glumly at the bedplate where the two-hundred-thousand-gallon Klenomatic ought to have been.

"He say anything when he took it away?" Clyde asked.

Morton shrugged and made a sour face.

"Yeah," said Clyde. He looked distastefully at a dead cigar and tossed it at the nearest oubliette. He missed.

"He said a month, two months," Morton told him. "You know what that means."

"Yeah."

"So I'll call up the factory," Morton said violently. "But I know what they're gonna tell me. Give us a deposit and we'll put you on a waiting list. *Waiting* list!"

"Yeah," said Clyde.

In a factory in Under Bronnix, the vice president in charge of sales shoved a thick folder of coded plastic slips under the nose of the vice president in charge of production. "Look at those orders," he said.

"Uh-huh," said Production.

"You know how far back they go? *Three years.* You know how much money this company's lost in unfilled orders? Over two million—"

"I *know*. What do you expect? Every fabricator in this place is too old. We're holding them together with spit and string. Don't bother me, will you, Harry. I got my own—"

"Listen," said Sales. "This can't go on much longer. It's up to us to tell the Old Man that he's got to try a bigger bribe on the Metals people. Mortgage the plant if we have to—it's the only thing to do."

"We have more mortgages now than the plant is worth."

Sales reddened. "Nick, this is serious. Last fall, it looked like we might squeeze through another year, but now... You know what's going to happen in another eight, ten months?" He snapped his fingers. "Right down the drain."

Production blinked at him wearily. "Bribes are no good any more, Harry. You know that as well as I do. They're out."

"Well, then what are we going to *do?*"

Production shook his head. "I don't know. I swear to God, I don't know."

Over in Metals Reclamation Four, in Under and Middle Jersey, the night shift was just beginning. In the blue-lit cavern of Ferrous, this involved two men, one bald and flabby, the other gray and gnarled. They exchanged a silent look, then each in turn put his face into the time clock's retinoscope mask. The clock, which had been emitting a shrill irritating sound, gurgled its satisfaction and shut up.

"Well, that's it," said the gray one. "I'll be your work gang and you be mine, huh?"

The flabby one spat. "Wonder what happened to Turk."

"Who cares? I never liked him."

"Just wondering. Yesterday he's here, today where is he? Labor pool, army—" he spat again, with care—"repair, maintenance... He was fifteen years in this department. I was just wondering."

"Scooping sewage, probably. That's about his speed." The gray man shambled over to the control bench opposite and looked at the indicators. Then he lighted a cigarette.

"Nothing in the hoppers?" the flabby one asked.

"Nah. They ought to put Turk in the hoppers. He had metal in his goddam teeth. Actual metal!"

"Turk wasn't old," the flabby one said reproachfully. "No more than sixty."

"I never liked him."

"First it was the kid—you know, Pimples. Then, lessee, the next one was that big guy, the realie actor—"

"Gustad. The hell with him."

"Yeah, Gustad. What I mean is, where do they go to? It's the same thing on my three-to-seven shift, over in Yeasts. Guys I know for ten, fifteen, twenty years on the same job. All of a sudden, they're gone and you never see them. Must be a hell of a thing, starting all over again somewhere else—guys like that—I mean you get set in your ways, kind of."

His eyes were patient and bewildered in their watery pouches. "Guys like me—no kids, nobody that gives a damn about 'em. Kind of gives you the jumps to think about it. You know what I mean?"

The gray one looked embarrassed, then irritated, then defiant. "Aah," he said, and produced a deck of cards from his kit—the grimy coating on the creaseless, frayless plastic as lovingly built and preserved as the patina in a meerschaum. "Cut for deal. Come on! Let's play."

"I'll have to know what you going to exhibit," the girl said. "For the Fair records."

"Labor-saving devices," Alvah told her, "the latest and best products of human ingenuity, designed to—"

"Machines," she said, writing. She added, looking up, "There's a fee for the use of the fairground space. Since you only going to have it for a day, we'll call it twenty twains."

Alvah hesitated. He had no idea what a twain might be—it had *sounded* like "twain." Evidently it was some sort of crude Muckfoot coinage.

"Afraid I haven't got any of your money," he said, producing a handful of steels from his belt change-meter. "I don't suppose these would do?"

The girl looked at him steadily. "Gold?" she said. "Precious stones, platinum, anything of that kind?" Alvah shook his head. "Sure?" Alvah shrugged despairingly. "Well," she said after a moment, "maybe something can be arranged. I'll let you talk to Doc about it, anyhow. He'll have to decide. Come on."

"Just a minute," Alvah said, and ducked back into the floater. He found what he was looking for and trotted outside again.

"What's that?" asked the girl, looking at the bulky kit at his waist.

"Just a few things I like to have with me."

"Mind showing me?"

"Well—no." He opened the kit. "Cigarette lighter, flashlight, shaver, raincoat, heater, a few medicines over here, jujubes, food concentrates, things like that. Uh, I don't know why I put this in here—it's a distress signal for people who get lost in the subway."

"You never can tell," said the girl, "when a thing like that will come in handy."

"That's true. Uh, this thing that looks like two dumbbells and a corkscrew..."

"Never mind," said the girl. "Come along."

The first shed they passed was occupied by things that looked like turtles with glittery four-foot shells. In the nearest stall, a man was peeling off from one of the beasts successive thin layers of this shell-stuff, which turned out to be colorless and transparent. He passed them to a woman, who dipped them into a basin and then laid them on a board to dry. The ones at the far end of the row, Alvah noticed, had flattened into discs.

The girl apparently misread his expression as curiosity. "Glass tortoise," she told him. "For windows and so on. The young ones have more hump to their shells—almost spherical to start with. Those are for bottles and bowls and things."

Alvah blinked noncommittally.

They passed a counter on which metal tools were displayed—knives, axes and the like. Similar objects, Alvah noted automatically, had only approximately similar outlines. There seemed to be no standardization at all.

"These are local," the girl said. "The metal comes from Iron Pits, just a few miles south of here."

In the next shed was a long row of upright rectangular frames, most of them empty. One near the end, however, was filled with some sort of insubstantial film or fabric. A tiny scarlet creature was crawling rapidly up and down this gossamer substance, working its way gradually from left to right.

"Squareweb," the girl informed him. "This dress I'm wearing was made that way."

Alvah verified his previous impression that the dress was opaque. Rather a pity, since it was also quite handsomely filled out. Not, he assured himself, that it made any difference—the girl was a Muckfoot, after all.

Next came a large cleared space. In it were half a dozen animals that resembled nothing in nature or nightmare except each other. They were wide and squat and at least six feet high at the shoulder. They had vaguely reptilian heads, and their scaly hides were patterned in orange and blue, rust and vermilion, yellow and poppy-red.

The oddest thing about them, barring the fact that each had three sets of legs, was the extraordinary series of protuberances that sprouted from their backs. First came an upright, slightly hollow shield sort of thing, set crossways behind the first pair of shoulders. Behind that, something that looked preposterously like an armchair—it even had a bright-colored cushion—and then a double row of upright spines with a wide space between them.

"Trucks," said the girl.

Alvah cleared his throat. "Look, Miss—"

"Betty Jane Hofmeyer. Call me B.J. Everybody does."

"All right—uh—B.J. I wonder if you could explain something to me. What's wrong with metal? And plastic, and things like that. I

mean why should you people want to go to so much trouble and —
and *mess,* when there are easier ways to do things better?"

"Each," she said, "to his own taste. We turn here."

A few yards ahead, the Fair ended and the settlement proper began with an unusually large building — large enough, Alvah esti-
mated, to fill almost an entire wing of a third-class hotel in New
York. Unlike the hovels he had seen farther south — which looked
as if they had been excreted — it was built of some regular, smooth-
surfaced material, seamless and fairly well shaped.

Alvah was so engrossed in these and other considerations that it
wasn't until the girl turned three steps inside the doorway, impatiently waiting, that he realized a minor crisis was at hand — he was
being invited to enter a Muckfoot dwelling.

"Well, come on," said B.J.

Refuse any offers of food, transportation, etc., said the handbook,
firmly, *but as diplomatically as possible. Employ whatever subterfuge the
situation may suggest, such as, "Thank you, but my doctor has forbidden
me to touch fur," or, "Pardon me, but I have a sore throat and am unable
to eat."*

Alvah cleared his throat frantically. The situation did not suggest
anything at all. Luckily, however, his stomach did.

"Maybe I'd better not come in," he said. "I don't feel very well.
Maybe if I just sit down here quietly —"

"You can sit down inside," said the girl briskly. "If there's anything wrong with you, Doc will look you over."

"Well," Alvah asked desperately, "couldn't you bring him out
here for a minute? I really don't think —"

"Doc is a busy man. Are you coming or not?"

Alvah hesitated. There were, he told himself, only two possibili-
ties, after all: (a) he would somehow manage to keep his breakfast,
and (b) he wouldn't.

The nausea began as a faint, premonitory twinge when he
stepped through the doorway. It increased steadily as he followed
B.J. past cages filled with things that chirruped, croaked, rumbled,

rustled or simply stared at him. The girl didn't invite comment on any of them, for which Alvah was grateful. He was too busy concentrating on trying not to concentrate on his misery.

For the same reason, he did not notice at what precise point the cages gave way to long rows of potted green plants. Alvah was just beginning to wonder if he would live to see the end of them when, still following B.J., he turned a corner and came upon a cleared space with half a dozen people in it.

One of them was the sad-faced youth, Artie. Another was a stocky man, all chest and paunch and no neck at all, who was talking to Artie while the others stood and listened. B.J. stopped and waited quietly. Alvah, perforce, did the same.

" —just a few seedlings and a couple of one-year-olds for now — we'll see how they go. If you have more room later on... What else was I going to tell you?" The stocky man rumpled his hair nervously. "Oh, look, Artie, I had a copy of the specifications for you, but the fool bird got into a fight with a mirror and broke his... Wait a second." He turned abruptly. "Hello, Beej. Come along to the library for a second, will you?"

He turned again and strode off, with Artie, B.J. and Alvah in his wake.

The room they entered was, from Alvah's point of view, the worst he had struck yet. It was a hundred feet long, by fifty wide, and everywhere — perched on the walls and on multi-leveled racks that ran the length of the room, darting through the air in flutters of brilliance — were tiny raucous birds, feathered in every prismatic shade, green, electric-blue, violet, screaming red.

"Mark seven one-oh-three!" Bither shouted. The roomful of birds took it up in a hideous echoing chorus. An instant later, a sudden flapping sound turned itself into an explosion of color and alighted on the stocky man's shoulder, preening its feathers with a blunt green beak. *"Rrk,"* it said and then, quite clearly, "Mark seven one-oh-three."

The stocky man made a perch of one forefinger and handed the thing across to Artie's shoulder. "I can't give you this one. It's the only copy I got. You'll have to listen to it and remember what you need."

"I'll remember." Artie glanced at the bird on his shoulder and said, "Magnus utility tree."

The stocky man looked around, saw B.J. "Now, Beej, is it important? Because—"

"Magnus utility tree," the bird was saying. "Thrive in all soils, over ninety-one per cent resistant to most rusts, scales and other infestations. Edible from root to branch. Young shoots and leaves excellent for salads. Self-fertilizing. Sap can be drawn in second year for—"

"Doc," said the girl clearly, "this is Alvah Gustad. From New York. Alvah, meet Doc Bither."

"—golden orangoes in spring and early summer, Bither aperries in late summer and fall. Will crossbreed with—"

"New York, huh?" said Bither. "You a long way from home, young—Excuse me. Artie?"

"—series five to one hundred fifteen. Trunks guaranteed straight and rectilinear, two-by-four at end of second year, four-by-six at—"

"I all set, Doc."

"—mealie pods and winterberries—"

"Fine, all right." He took B.J.'s arm. "Let's go someplace we can talk."

"—absorb fireproofing and stiffening solution freely through roots..."

Bither led the way into a small, crowded room. "Now," he said, peering intently at Alvah, "what's the problem?"

B.J. explained briefly. Then they both stared at Alvah. Sweat was beaded coldly on his brow and his knees were trembling, but he seemed to have stabilized the nausea just below the critical point. The idea, he told himself, was to convince yourself that the whole building was a realie stage and all the objects in it props. Wasn't there a line to that effect in one of the classics – *The Manager of Copenhagen*, or perhaps *Have It Your Own Way?*

"What do you think?" Bither asked.

"Might try him out."

"Um. Damn it, I wish we hadn't run out of birds. Can you take this down for me, Beej? I'll arrange for the Fair rental fee, Alvah, if you just answer a few questions."

It sounded innocuous enough but Alvah felt a twinge of suspicion. "What kind of questions?"

"Just personal questions, like how old, what you do for a living."

"Twenty-six. I'm an actor."

"Always been an actor?"

"No."

"What else you done?"

"Labor."

"What kind?" B.J. asked.

"Worked with his hands, he means," Bither told her. "Parents laborers, too?"

"Yes."

B.J. and Bither exchanged glances. Alvah shifted uncomfortably. "If that's all..."

"One or two more. I want you to tell me, near as you can, when was the first time you remember knowing that our clothes and our animals and us and all the things we make smelled bad?"

It was too much. Alvah turned and lurched blindly out the door. He heard their voices behind him:

"...minutes."

"...alley door!"

Then there were hands on him, steering him from behind as he stumbled forward at a half-run. They turned him right, then left and finally he was out in the cool air, not a moment too soon.

When he straightened, wiping tears away, he was alone, but a moment later the girl appeared in the doorway.

"That's all," she said distantly. "You can start your exhibition whenever you want."

IV

The magic tricks went over fairly well — at least nobody yawned. The comic monologue, however, was a flat failure, even though the piece had been expertly slanted for a rural audience and, by all the laws of psychostatics, should have rated at least half a dozen boffs. ("So the little boy came moseying back up the road, and his grandpa said to him, 'Why didn't you drive them hogs out of the corn like I told you?' And the little fellow piped up, 'Them ain't hogs — them's shoats!'")

Alvah launched hopefully into his sales talks and demonstrations.

The all-purpose fireless lifetime cooker was received with blank stares. When Alvah fried up a savory batch of protein-paste fritters and offered to hand them out, nobody responded but one small boy, and his mother hauled him down off the platform stair by the slack of his pants.

Smiling doggedly, Alvah brought out the pocket-workshop power tools and accessories. This, it appeared, was more like it. An interested hum went up as he drilled three holes of various sizes in a bar of duroplast, then sawed through it from end to end and finally cut a mortise in one piece, a tenon in the other, and fitted them together. A few more people drifted in.

"And now, friends," said Alvah, "if you'll continue to give me your kind attention..."

The next item was the little giant power-plant for the home, shop or office. Blank stares again. Alvah picked out one Muckfoot in the front row — a blear-eyed, open-mouthed fellow, with hair over his forehead and a basket under his arm, who seemed typical—and spoke directly to him. He outdid himself about the safety, economy, efficiency and unobtrusiveness of a little giant power-plant. He explained its operation in words a backward two-year-old could understand.

"A little giant," he concluded, leaning over the platform rail to stare hypnotically into the Muckfoot's eyes, "is the power-plant for *you!*"

The fellow blinked, slowly produced a dark-brown lump of something from his pocket, slowly put it into his inattentive mouth, and as slowly began to chew.

Alvah breathed deeply and clutched the rail. "And now," he said, giving the clincher, "the marvel of the age—the super-speed runabout!" He pressed the button that popped open a segment of the floater's hull and lowered the gleaming little two-wheeled car into view.

"Now, friends," he said, "just to demonstrate the amazing qualities of this miracle of modern science—is there any gentleman in the crowd who has an animal he fancies for speed?"

For the first time, the Muckfeet reacted according to the charts. Shouts rocketed up: "Me, by damn!" "Me!" "Right here, mister!" "Yes, sir!"

"Friends, friends!" said Alvah, spreading his hands. "There won't be time to accommodate you all. Choose one of you to represent the rest!"

"*Swifty!*" somebody yelped, and other voices took up the cry. A red-haired young man began working his way back out of the crowd, propelled by gleeful shouts and slaps on the back.

Alvah took an indicator and began pointing out the salient features of the runabout. He had not got more than a quarter of the way through when the redhead reappeared, mounted astride an animal which, to Alvah's revolted gaze, looked to be part horse, part lynx, part camel and part pure horror.

To the crowd, evidently, it was one of nature's finest efforts. Alvah swallowed bile and raised his voice again. "Clear a space now, friends—all the way around!"

It took time, but eventually self-appointed deputies began to get the crowd moving. Alvah descended, carrying two bright marker poles, and, followed by the inquisitive redhead, set one up at either side of the enclosure, a few yards short of the boundary.

"This will be the course," he told Swifty. "Around these markers and the floater—that thing I was standing on. We'll do ten laps, starting and finishing here. Is that all right?"

"All right with me," said the redhead, grinning more widely than before.

There were self-appointed time-keepers and starters, too. When Alvah, in the runabout, and the redhead, on his monster, were satisfactorily lined up, one of them bellowed, "On y' marks—Git set..." and then cracked a short whip with a noise out of all proportion to its size.

For a moment, Alvah thought Swifty and his horrid mount had simply disappeared. Then he spotted them, diminished by perspective, halfway down the course, and rapidly getting smaller. He slammed the power bar over and took off in pursuit.

Around the first turn, it was Swifty, with Alvah nowhere. In the stretch, Alvah was coming up fast on the outside. Around the far turn, he was two monster lengths behind and, in the stretch again, they were neck and neck. Alvah kept it that way for the next two laps and then gradually pulled ahead. The crowd became a multicolored streak, whirling past him. In the sixth lap, he passed Swifty again—in the eighth, again—in the tenth, still again—and when he skidded to a halt beyond the finish post, fluttering its flags with the wind of his passage, poor old Swifty and his steaming beast were still lumbering halfway down the stretch.

"Now, friends," said Alvah, triumphantly mounting the platform again, "in a moment, I'm going to tell you how you, yourselves, can own this wonderful runabout and many marvels more—but first, are there any questions you'd like to ask?"

Swifty pushed forward, grinless, looking like a man smitten by lightning. "How many to a get?" he called.

Alvah decided he must have misunderstood. "You can have any number you want," he said. "The price is so reasonable—but I'm going to come to that in a—"

"I don't mean how many will you *sell*. How many calves, or colts, or whatever, is what I want to know."

There was a general murmur of agreement. This, it would seem, was what everybody wanted to know.

Appalled, Alvah corrected the misapprehension as quickly and clearly as he could.

"Mean to say," somebody called, "they don't *breed?*"

"Certainly not. If one of them ever breaks down—and, friends, they're built to last—you get it repaired or buy another."

"How much?" somebody in the crowd yelled.

"Friends, I'm not here to take your money," Alvah said. "We just want—"

"Then how we going to pay for your stuff?"

"I'm coming to that. When two people want to trade, friends, there's usually a way. You want our products. We want metals— iron, aluminum, chromium—"

"Suppose a man ain't got any metal?"

"Well, sir, there are a lot of other things we can use besides metal. Natural fruits and vegetables, for instance."

The slack-faced yokel in the first row, the one with the basket under his arm, roused himself for the first time. His mouth closed, then opened again. "*What* kind?"

"Natural products, friend. You know, the kind your great-granddad ate. We use a lot every year for table delicacies, even—"

The yokel came halfway up the platform stair. His gnarled fingers dipped into the basket and came up with a smooth red-gold ovoid. He shoved it toward Alvah. "You mean," he said incredulously, "you wouldn't eat *that?*"

Gulping, Alvah backed away a step. The Muckfoot came after him. "Raise 'em myself," he said plaintively, holding out the red fruit. "I tell you, they just the juiciest, goodest—Go ahead, try one."

"I'm not hungry," Alvah said desperately. "I'm on a diet. Now if you'll just step down quietly, friend, till after the—"

The Muckfoot stared at him, holding the fruit under Alvah's nose. "You mean you won't *try* it?"

"No," said Alvah, trying not to breathe. "Now go on back down there, friend—don't crowd me."

"Well," said the Muckfoot, "then durn you!" And he shoved the disgusting thing squashily into Alvah's face.

Alvah saw red. Blinking away a glutinous film of juice and pulp, he glimpsed the yokel's face, spread into a hideous grin. Waves of laughter beat about his ears. Retching, he brought up his right fist in an instinctive roundhouse swing that clapped the yokel's grin shut and toppled him over the platform rail, basket, flying fruit and all.

The laughter rumbled away into expectant silence. Alvah fumbled in his kit for tissues, scrubbed a wad of them across his face and saw them come away daubed with streaky red. He hurled them convulsively into the crowd and, leaning over the rail, shouted thickly, "Lousy stinking filthy *Muckfeet!*"

Muckfoot men in the front ranks turned and looked at each other solemnly. Then two of them marched up the platform stair and, behind them, another two.

Still berserk, Alvah met the first couple with two violent kicks in the chest. This cleared the stair, but he turned to find three more candidates swarming over the rail. He swung at the nearest, who ducked. The next one seized Alvah's arm with both hands and toppled over backward. Alvah followed, head foremost, and landed with a jar that shook him to his toes.

The next thing he knew, he was lying on the ground surrounded by upward of twenty thick seamless boots, choking on dust, and getting the daylights methodically kicked out of him.

Alvah rolled over frantically, climbed the first leg that came to hand, got his back against the platform and, by dint of cracking skulls together, managed in two brisk minutes to clear a momentary space around him. Another dim figure lunged at him. Alvah clouted it under the ear, whirled and vaulted over the rail onto the platform.

His gun popped out into his hand.

For just a moment, he was standing alone, feeling the pistol grip clenched hard in his dirt-caked palm and able to judge exactly how long he had before half a dozen Muckfeet would swarm up the stair and over the rail. The crowd's faces were sharp and clear. He saw Artie and Doc Bither and Jake, his mouth open to howl, and he saw the girl, B.J., in a curious posture—leaning forward, her right arm thrust out and down. She looked as if she had just thrown something.

Alvah saw the gray-white blur wobbling toward him. He tried to dodge, but the thing struck his shoulder and exploded with a papery pop. For an instant, the air was full of dancing bright particles. Then they were gone.

Alvah didn't have time to wonder about it. He thumbed the selector over to *Explosive,* pointed the gun straight up and squeezed the trigger.

Nothing happened.

There were two Muckfeet half over the rail and three more coming up the stair. Incredulous, still aiming at the air, Alvah tried again—and again. The gun didn't work.

Three Muckfeet were on the platform, four more right behind them. Alvah spun through the open door and slapped at the control button. The door stayed open.

The Muckfeet were massed in the doorway, staring in like visitors at an aquarium. Alvah dived at the power bar, shoved it over. The floater didn't lift.

"Holly! Luke!" called a clear voice outside, and the Muckfeet turned. "Leave him alone. He's got enough troubles now."

Alvah was pawing at the control board.

The lights didn't work.

The air-conditioner didn't work.

The scent-organ didn't work.

The musivox didn't work.

One of the Muckfeet put his head in at the door. "Reckon he has," he said thoughtfully and went away again. Alvah heard his voice, more faintly. "You do something, B.J.?"

"Yes," said the girl, "I did something."

Moving warily, Alvah went outside. The girl was standing just below the platform, watching as the Muckfoot men filed down the stair.

"You!" he said to her.

She paid him no attention. "Just one of those things, Luke," she said.

Luke nodded solemnly. "Well, the Fair don't come but once a year." He and the other men moved past her into the crowd, each one acquiring a train of curiosity-seekers as he went. The crowd began to drift away.

A familiar voice yelped, "Ride'm out on a *razorback* is what *I* say!"

A chorus of "Now, Jake!" went up. There were murmurs of dissent, of inquiry, of explanation. "Time for the poultry judging!" somebody called, and the crowd moved faster.

Alvah went dazedly down and climbed into the runabout. He waggled its power bar. No response.

He tore open his kit and began frantically hauling out one glittering object after another, holding each for an instant and then throwing it on the ground. The razor, the heater, the vacuum cleaner, the sonotube, the vibromasseur.

Swifty rode by, at ease atop his horse-lynx-camel-horror. He was whistling.

The crowd was almost gone. Among the stragglers was Jake, fists on his pudgy hips, his choleric cheeks gleaming with sweat and satisfaction.

"Well, Mister High-and-Mighty," he called, "what you going to do *now?*"

That was just what Alvah was wondering. He was about a thousand miles from home by air—probably more like fifteen hundred across-country. He had no transportation, no shelter, no power tools, no equipment. He had, he realized with horror, been cut off instantly from everything that made a man civilized.

What *was* he going to do?

V

Manager Wytak had his feet on the glossy desktop. So did the Comptroller, narrow-faced old Mr. Creedy; the Director of Information, plump Mr. Kling; the Commissioner of Supply, blotched and pimpled Mr. Jackson; and the porcine Mr. McArdle, Commissioner of War. With chairs tilted back, they stared through a haze of cigar smoke at each others' stolid faces mirrored on the ceiling.

Wytak's voice was as confident as ever, if a trifle muted, and when the others spoke, he listened. These were not the hired nonentities Alvah had seen; these were the men who had made Wytak, the electorate with whose consent he governed.

"Jack," said Wytak, "I want you to look at it my way and see if you don't think I'm right. It isn't a question of how long we can hold out—when you get right down and look at it, it's a question of *can we do anything.*"

"In time," said Jackson expressionlessly.

"In time. But if we can do anything, there'll be time enough. You say we've got troubles now and you're right, but I tell you we can pull through a situation a thousand times worse than this—*if* we've got an answer. And have we got an answer? We have."

Creedy grunted. "Like to see some results, Boley."

"You'll see them. You can't skim a yeast tank the first day, Will."

"You can see the bubbles, though," said Jackson sourly. "Any report from this Gustad today, while we're talking about it?"

"Not yet. He was getting some response yesterday. He's following it up. I trust that boy—the analyzers picked his card out of five million. Wait and see. He'll deliver."

"If you say so, Boley."

"I say so."

Jackson nodded. "That's good enough. Gentlemen?"

In another soundproof, spyproof office in Over Manhattan, Kling and McArdle met again twenty minutes later.

"What do you think?" asked Kling with his meaningless smile.

"Moderately good. I was hoping he would lie about Gustad's report, but of course there was very little chance of that. Wytak is an old hand."

"You admire him?" Kling suggested.

"As a specimen of his type. Wytak pulled us out of a very bad spot in '39."

"Agreed."

"And he has had his uses since then. There are times when brilliant improvisation is better than sound principles—and times when it is not. Wytak is an incurable romantic."

"And you?"

"We," said McArdle grimly, "are realists."

"Oh, yes. But perhaps *we* are not anything just yet. Creedy is interested, but not convinced—and until he moves, Jackson will do nothing."

"Wytak's project is a failure. You can't do business with the Muckfeet. But the fool was so confident that he didn't even interfere with Gustad's briefing."

Kling leaned forward with interest. "You didn't...?"

"*No.* It wasn't necessary. But it means that Gustad has no instructions to fake successful reports—and that means Wytak can't stall until he gets back. There was no report today. Suppose there's none tomorrow, or the next day, or the next."

"In that case, of course... However, it's always as well to offer something positive. You said you might have something to show me today."

"Yes. Follow me."

In a sealed room at the end of a guarded corridor, five young men were sitting. They leaped to attention when Kling and McArdle entered.

"At ease," said McArdle. "This gentleman is going to ask you some questions. You may answer freely." He turned to Kling. "Go ahead — ask them anything."

Kling's eyebrows went up delicately, but he looked the young men over, selected one and said, "Your name?"

"Walter B. Limler, sir."

Kling looked mildly pained. "Please don't call me sir. Where do you live?"

"CFF Barracks, Tier Three, McCormick."

"CFF?" said Kling with a frown. "McCormick? I don't place the district. Where is it?"

The young man, who was blond and very earnest, allowed himself to show a slight surprise. "In the Loop," he said.

"And where is the Loop?"

The young man looked definitely startled. He glanced at McArdle, moistened his lips and said, "Well, right here, sir. In Chicago."

Kling's eyebrows went up and then down. He smiled. "I begin to see," he murmured to McArdle.

It cost Alvah two hours' labor, using tools that had never been designed to be operated manually, to get the inspection plate off the motor housing in the floater. He compared the intricate mechanism with the diagrams and photographs in the maintenance handbook. He looked for dust and grime; he checked the moving parts for play; he probed for dislodged wiring plates and corrosion. He did everything the handbook suggested, even spun the flywheel and was positive he felt the floater lift a fraction of an inch beneath him. As far as he could tell, there was absolutely nothing wrong, unless the trouble was in the core of the motor itself — the force-field that rotated the axle that made everything go.

The core casing had an "easily removable" segment, meaning to say that Alvah was able to get it off in three hours more.

Inside, there was no resistance to his cautious finger. The spool-shaped hollow space was empty.

Under *Motor Force-field Inoperative* the manual said simply: *Remove and replace rhodopalladium nodules.*

Alvah looked. He found the tiny sockets where the nodules ought to be, one in the flanged axle-head, the other facing it at the opposite end of the chamber. The nodules were not there at all.

Alvah went into the storage chamber. Ignoring the increasingly forceful protests of his empty stomach, he spent a furious twenty minutes locating the spare nodules. He stripped the seal off the box and lifted the lid.

There were the nodules. And there, appearing out of nowhere, was a whirling cloud of brightness that settled briefly in the box and then went back where it came from. And there the nodules weren't.

Alvah stared at the empty box. He poked his forefinger into the cushioned niches, one after the other. Then he set the box down with care, about-faced, walked outside to the platform and sat down on the top step with his chin on his fists.

"You looked peaked," said B.J.'s firm voice.

Alvah looked up at her briefly. "Go away."

"Had anything to eat today?" the girl asked.

Alvah did not reply.

"Don't sulk," she said. "You've got a problem. We feel responsible. Maybe there's something we can do to help."

Alvah stood up slowly. He looked her over carefully, from head to toe and back again. "There is one thing you could do for me," he said. "Smile."

"Why?" she asked cagily.

"I just wanted to see your fangs." He turned wearily and went into the floater.

He puttered around for a few minutes, then got cold rations out of the storage chamber and sat down in the control chair to eat them. But the place was odious to him with its gleaming, useless array of gadgetry, and he went outside again and sat down with his back to the hull near the doorway. The girl was still there, looking up at him.

"Look," she said, "I'm sorry about this."

The nutloaf went down his gullet in one solid lump and hit his stomach like a stone. "Please don't mention it," he said bitterly. "It was really nothing at all."

"I had to do it. You might have killed somebody."

Alvah tried another bite. Chewing the stuff, at any rate, gave him something to do. "What *were* those things?" he demanded.

"Metallophage," she said. "They eat metals in the platinum family. Hard to get them that selective—we weren't exactly sure what would happen."

Alvah put down the remnant of nutloaf slowly. "Who's 'we'? You and Bither?"

"Mostly."

"And you—you bred those things to eat rhodopalladium?"

She nodded.

"Then you must have some to feed them," said Alvah logically. He stood up and gripped the railing. "Give it to me."

She hesitated. "There might be some—"

"*Might* be? There *must* be!"

"You don't understand. They don't actually eat the metal—not for nourishment, that is."

"Then what do they do with it?"

"They build nests," she told him. "But come on over to the lab and we'll see."

At the laboratory door, they were still arguing. "For the last time," said Alvah, "I will not come in. I've just eaten half a nutcake and I haven't got any food to waste. Get the stuff and bring it out."

"For the last time," said B.J., "get it out of your head that what you want is all that counts. If you want me to look for the metal, you'll come in, and that's flat."

They glared at each other. Well, he told himself resignedly, he hadn't wanted that nutloaf much in the first place.

They followed the same route, past the things that chirruped, croaked, rumbled, rustled. The main thing, he recalled, was to keep your mind off it.

"Tell me something," he said to her trim back. "If I hadn't got myself mixed up with that farmer and his market basket, do you still think I wouldn't have sold anything?"

"That's right."

"Well, why not? Why all this resistance to machinery? Is it a taboo of some kind?"

She said nothing for a moment.

"Is it because you're afraid the Cities will get a hold on you?" Alvah insisted. "Because that's foolish. Our interests are really the same as yours. We don't just want to sell you stuff—we want to help you help yourselves. The more prosperous you get, the better for us."

"It's not that," she said.

"Well, what then? It's been bothering me. You've got all these raw materials, all this land. You wouldn't have to wait for us—you could have built your own factories, made your own machines. But you never have. I can't understand why."

"It's not worth the trouble."

He choked. "*Anything* is worth the trouble, if it helps you do the same work more efficiently, more intel—"

"Wait a minute." She stopped a woman who was passing in the aisle between the cages. "Marge, where's Doc?"

"Down in roundworms, I think."

"Tell him I have to see him, will you? It's urgent. We'll wait in here." She led the way into a windowless room, as small and cluttered as any Alvah had seen.

"Now," she said. "We don't make a fuss about machines because most people simply haven't any need for them."

"That's ridiculous," Alvah argued. "You may think—"

"Be quiet and let me finish. We haven't got centralized industries or power installations. Why do you think the Cities have never beaten us in a war, as often as they've tried? Why do you think we've taken over the whole world, except for twenty-two Cities? You've got to face this sooner or later—in every single respect, *our plants and animals are more efficient than any machine you could build.*"

Alvah inspected her closely. Her eyes were intent and brilliant. Her bosom indicated deep and steady breathing. To all appearance, she was perfectly serious.

"Nuts," he replied with dignity.

B.J. shook her head impatiently. "I know you've got a brain. Use it. What's the most expensive item that goes into a machine?"

"Metal. We're a little short of it, to tell the truth."

"Think again. What are all your gadgets supposed to save?"

"Well, labor."

"Human labor. If metal is expensive, it's because it costs a lot of man-hours."

"If you want to look at it that way—"

"It's true, isn't it? Why is a complicated thing more expensive than a simple one? More man-hours to make it. Why is a rare thing more expensive than a common one? More man-hours to find it. Why is a—"

"All right, what's your point?"

"Take your runabout. You saw that was the thing that interested people most, but I'll show you why you never could have sold one. How many man-hours went into manufacturing it?"

Alvah shifted restlessly. "It isn't in production. It's a trade item."

She sniffed. "Suppose it was in production. Make an honest guess. Figure in everything—amortization on the plant and equipment, materials, labor and so on. You can check your answer against wages and prices in your own money—you'll come pretty close."

Alvah reflected. "Between seven-fifty and a thousand."

"Compare that with Swifty's Morgan Gamma—the thing you raced against. Two man-hours—just two, and I'm being generous."

"Interesting," said Alvah, "if true." He suppressed an uneasy belch.

"Figure it out. An hour for the vet when he was foaled. Call it another hour for amortization on the stable where it happened, but that's too much. It isn't hard to grow a stable and they last a long time."

Alvah, who had been holding his own as long as machines were the topic, wasn't sure he could keep it up—or, more correctly, down. "All right, two hours," he said. "The animals feed themselves and water themselves, no doubt."

"They do, but that comes under upkeep. Our animals forage, most of them—all the big ones. The rest are cheap and easy to feed. Your machines have to be fueled. Our animals repair themselves, like any living organism, only better and faster. Your machines have to be repaired and serviced. More man-hours. Incidentally, if you and Swifty took a ten-hour trip, you in your runabout, him on his Morgan, you'd spend just ten hours steering. Swifty would spend maybe fifteen minutes all told. And now we come to the payoff—"

"Some other time," said Alvah irritably.

"This is important. When your runabout—"

"I'd rather not talk about it any more," said Alvah, raising his voice. "Do you *mind?*"

"When your runabout breaks down and can't be fixed," she said firmly, "you have to buy another. Swifty's mare drops twins every year. There. Think about it."

The door opened and Bither came in, looking more disheveled than ever. "Hello, Beej, Alvah. Beej, I think we shoulda used annelid stock for this job. These F_3 batches no good at—you two arguing?"

Alvah recovered himself with an effort. "Rhodopalladium," he said thickly. "I need about a gram. Have you got it?"

"Not a scrap," said Bither cheerfully. "Except in the nests, of course."

"I told him I didn't think so," B.J. said.

Alvah closed his eyes for a second. "Where," he asked carefully, "are the nests?"

"Wish I knew," Bither admitted. "It's frustrating as hell. You see, we had to make them awful small and quick, the metallophage. Once you let them out of the sacs, there's no holding them. We did so good a job, we can't check to see how good a job we did." He rubbed his chin thoughtfully. "Of course, that's beside the point. Even if we had the metals, how would you get the alloy you need?"

"Palladium," said the girl, "melts at fifteen fifty-three Centigrade. I asked the hand bird."

"Best we can get out of a salamander is about six hundred," Bither added. "Isn't good for them, either—they get esophagitis."

"And necrosis," the girl said, watching Alvah intently.

His eyes were watering. It was hard to see. "Are you telling—"

"We're trying to tell you," she said, "that you can't go back. You've got to start getting used to the idea. There isn't a thing you can do except settle down here and learn to live with us."

Alvah could feel his jaw working, but no words were coming out. The bulge of nausea in his middle was squeezing its way inexorably upward.

Somebody grabbed his arm. "In there!" said Bither urgently.

A door opened and closed behind him, and he found himself facing a hideous white-porcelain antique with a pool of water in it. There was a roaring in his ears, but before the first spasm took him, he could hear the girl's and Bither's voices faintly from the other room:

"Eight minutes that time."

"Beej, I don't know."

"We can *do* it!"

"Well, I suppose we can, but can we do it before he starves?"

There was a sink in the room, but Alvah would sooner have drunk poison. He fumbled in his disordered kit until he found the condenser canteen. He rinsed out his mouth, took a tonus capsule and a mint lozenge. He opened the door.

"Feeling better?" asked the girl.

Alvah stared at her, retched feebly and fled back into the wash-room.

When he came out again, Bither said, "He's had enough, Beej. Let's take him out in the courtyard till he gets his strength back."

They moved toward him. Alvah said weakly, but with feeling, "Keep your itchy hands off me." He walked unsteadily past them, turned when he reached the doorway. "I hate to urp and run, but I'll never forget your hospitality. If there's ever anything I can do for you—anything at all—please hesitate to call on me."

He heard muttering voices and an odd scraping sound behind him, but he didn't look back. He was halfway down the aisle be-tween the cages when something furry and gray scuttled into view and sat up, grinning at him.

It looked like an ordinary capuchin monkey except for its head, which was grotesquely large. "Go away," said Alvah. He advanced with threatening gestures. The thing chattered at him and stayed where it was.

The aisle behind him was deserted. Very well, there were other exits. Alvah followed his nose back into the plant section and turned right.

There was the monkey-thing again.

At the next intersection of aisles, there were two of them. Alvah turned left.

And right.

And left.

And emerged into a large empty space enclosed by buildings.

"This is the courtyard," said Bither, coming forward with the girl behind him. "Now be reasonable, Alvah. You want to get back to New York, don't you?"

This did not seem to call for comment. Alvah stared at him in silence.

"Well," said Bither, "there's just one way you can do it. It won't be easy—I don't even say you got more than a fighting chance. One thing, though—it's up to you just how hard you make it for yourself."

"Get to the point," Alvah said.

"You got to let us decondition you so you can eat our food, ride on our animals. Now *think* about it, don't just—"

Alvah swung around, looking for the fastest and most direct exit. Before he had time to find it, a dizzying thought struck him and he turned back.

"Is that what this whole thing has been about?" he demanded. He glared at Bither, then at B.J. "Is that the reason you were so helpful? *Did you engineer that fight?*"

Bither clucked unhappily. "Would we admit it if we did? Alvah, I'll admit this much—of course we interested in you for our own reasons. This is the first time in thirty years we had a chance to study a City man. But what I just told you is true. If you want to get back home, this is your only chance."

"Then I'm a dead man," said Alvah.

"You is if you think you is," Bither told him. "Beej, you try."

She looked at Alvah levelly. "You think what we suggesting isn't possible. Right? Of course, we could do it. But I guess you already realize that your people are backward compared to us."

Half angry, half curious, Alvah demanded, "Just how do you figure that?"

"Easy. You probably don't know much biology, but you must know this much. What's the one quality that makes human beings the dominant race on this planet?"

Alvah snorted. "Are you trying to tell me I'm not as bright as a Muckfoot?"

"Not intelligence. Try again. Something more general—intelligence is only a special phase of it."

Alvah's patience was narrowing to a brittle thread. *"You* tell *me."*

"All right. We like to think intelligence is important, but you can't argue that way. It's special pleading—the way a whale might argue that size is the measuring stick, or a microbe might say numbers. But—"

"Control of environment," Alvah said.

"Right. Another name for it is adaptability. No other organism is so independent of environment, so adaptable as Man. And we could live in New York if we had to, just as we can live in the Arctic Circle or the tropics. And since you don't dare even try to live here..."

"All right," Alvah said bitterly, after a moment. "When do we start?"

VI

He refused to be hypnotized.

"You promised to help," B.J. said in annoyance. "We can't break the conditioning till we find out how it was done, you big oaf!"

"The whole thing is ridiculous anyhow," Alvah pointed out. "I said I'd let you try and I will—you can prod me around to your heart's content—but not that. I've put in a lot of Required Contribution time in restricted laboratories. Military secrets. How do I know you wouldn't ask me about those if you got me under?"

"We're not *interested* in—" B.J. began furiously, but Bither cut her off.

"We is, though, Beej. Might be important for us to know what kind of defenses New York has built up, and I was going to ask him if I got the chance." He sighed. "Well, there is other ways to skin a glovebeast. Lean back and relax, Alvah."

"No tricks?" Alvah asked suspiciously.

"No, we just going to try to improve your conscious recall. Relax now; close your eyes. Now think of a room, one that's familiar to you, and describe it to me. Take your time... Now we going further back—further back. You three years old and you just dropped something on the floor. What is it?"

Bither seemed to know what he was doing, Alvah had to admit. Day after day they dredged up bits and scraps of memory from his childhood, events he had forgotten so completely that he would almost have sworn they had never happened. At first, all of them seemed trivial and irrelevant, but even so, Alvah found, there was an unexpected fascination in this search through the dusty attics of his mind. Once they hit something that made Bither sit up sharply—a dark figure holding something furry, and an accompanying remembered stench.

Whether or not it had been as important as Bither seemed to think, they never got it back again. But they did get other things—an obscene couplet about the Muckfeet that had been popular in P. S. 9073 when Alvah was ten; a scene from a realie feature called *Nix on the Stix;* a whispered horror story; a frightening stereo picture in a magazine.

"What we have to do," B.J. told him at one point, "is to make you realize that none of this was your own idea. They *made* you feel this way. They did it to you."

"Well, I know that," said Alvah.

She stared at him in astonishment. "You knew it all along—and you don't care?"

"No." Alvah felt puzzled and irritated. "Why should I?"

"Don't you think they should have let you make up your own mind?"

Alvah considered this. "You have to make your children see things the way you do, otherwise there wouldn't be any continuity from one generation to the next. You couldn't keep any kind of civilization going. Where would we be if we let people wander off into the Sticks and become Muckfeet?"

He finished triumphantly, but she didn't look crushed. She merely grinned with an exasperating air of satisfaction and said, "Why should they want to—unless we can give them a better life than the Cities can?"

This was absurd, but Alvah couldn't find the one answer that would flatten her, no matter how long and often he mulled it over. Meanwhile, his tolerance of Muckfoot dwellings progressed from ten minutes to thirty, to an hour, to a full day. He didn't like it and nothing, he knew could ever make him like it, but he could stand it. He was able to ride for short distances on Muckfoot animals, and he was even training himself to wear an animal-hide belt for longer and longer periods each day. But he still couldn't eat Muckfoot food—the bare thought of it still nauseated him—and his own supplies were running short.

Oddly, he didn't feel as anxious about it as he should have. He could sense the resistance within him softening day by day. He was irrationally sure that that last obstacle would go, too, when the time came. Something else was bothering him, something he couldn't even name—but he dreamed of it at night and its symbol was the threatening vast arch of the sky.

Gradually, from Bither and B.J. and occasionally from some of the other lab workers, Alvah got a picture of the way Muckfoot biogenetics had developed. He had never spent much time wondering how the Muckfeet created their obscene animals and plants; it wasn't something you enjoyed thinking about. He still didn't like it; but, he discovered, there was more to it than you would expect.

Working with exact gene charts and with the Jenkins-Scripture surgical techniques, Muckfoot geneticists could combine or alter characteristics at will. They could overcome the incompatibility of widely different organisms, producing unlikely hybrids of ant and lobster, cat and dog, elm and asparagus. By these methods, and by controlled mutation, they were able to tailor living organisms for any use. In just under a century, they had created a whole new biota, from soil bacteria to draught animals.

Bither thought the science was still in its infancy. He forecast a day when the present rural existence of the Muckfeet would give way to a sort of garden city pattern: when even such farm labor as the Muckfeet did would be eliminated, and highly versatile and sophisticated living organisms would serve every need.

"No reason why you got to have two different plants for shelter and food," he said. "Some day we'll eat fruit from the walls of our houses. Another thing, there's nothing in the plasm that say you can't restructure the adult zygote. We might be able to build in trigger responses that would change part of an organism into something else when we need it. Save all the development and growth time. We just beginning now, Alvah. You wait and see, twenty, thirty years from now."

It all had a sort of horrid fascination. He couldn't help being interested in the fine structure that disclosed itself as he got deeper into the subject. But he didn't like it, and he never would.

After the Fair was over, it seemed that B.J. had very little work to do. As far as Alvah could make out, the same was true of everybody. The settlement grew mortuary-still. For an hour or so every morning, lackadaisical trading went on in the central market place. In the evenings, sometimes, there was music of a sort and a species of complicated ungainly folk-dancing. The rest of the time, children raced through the streets and across the pastures, playing incomprehensible games. Their elders, when they were visible, sat — on doorsteps by ones and twos, grouped on porches and lawns — their hands busy, oftener than not, with some trifle of carving or needlework, but their faces as blank and sleepy as a frog's in the Sun.

"What do you do for excitement around here?" he asked B.J. in a dither of boredom.

She looked at him oddly. "We work. We make things, or watch things grow. But maybe that's not the kind of excitement you mean."

"It isn't, but let it go."

"Our simple pleasures probably wouldn't interest you," she said reflectively. "They're pretty dull. We dance, go riding, swim in the lake..."

So they swam.

It wasn't bad. It was unsettling to have no place to swim *to* — you had to head out from the shore, gauging your distance, and then turn around to go back — but the lake, to Alvah's considerable surprise, was clearer and better-tasting than any pool he'd ever been in.

Lying on the grass afterward was a novel sensation, too. It was comfortable — no, it was nothing of the sort; the grass blades prickled and the ground was lumpy. Not comfortable, but — comforting.

It was the weight, he thought lazily, the massive mother-weight of the whole Earth cradling you—the endless slow pendulum-swing you felt when you closed your eyes.

He sat up, feeling cheerfully torpid. B.J. was lying on her back beside him, eyes shut, one arm flung back behind her head. It was a graceful pose. In a detached way, he admired it, first in general and then in particular—the fine texture of her skin, the firmness of her bosom under the halter that half-covered it, the delicate tint of her closed eyelids—the catalogue prolonged itself, and he realized that B.J., when you got a good look at her, was a lovely girl. He wondered, in passing, how he had missed noticing it before.

She opened her eyes and looked at him. There was a ground-swell of some sort and, without particular surprise, Alvah found himself kissing her.

"Beej," he said some time later, "when I go back to New York—I don't suppose you'd want to come with me? I mean—you're different from the others. You're educated, you can read; even your grammar is good."

"I know you mean it as a compliment and I'm doing my best not to sound ungrateful or hurt your feelings, but..." She made a frustrated gesture. "Take the reading—that's a hobby of Doc's and I picked it up from him. It's a primitive skill, Alvah, something like manuscript illuminating. We have better ways now. We don't *need* it any more. Then the grammar—didn't it ever strike you that I might be using your kind just to make things easier for you?"

She frowned. "I guess that was a mistake. As of now, I quit. No, listen a minute! The only difference between your grammar and ours is that yours is sixty years out of date. You still use 'I am, you are, he is' and all that archaic nonsense of person and number. What for? If that's good, suppose we hunted up somebody who said 'I am, thou art, he is,' would his grammar be better than yours?"

"Well—" said Alvah.

"And about New York, I appreciate that. But the Cities are done for, Alvah. In ten years there won't be one left. They're *finished*."

Alvah stiffened. "That's the most ridiculous—"

"*Is* it? Then why you here?"

"Well, we're in a crisis period now, but we've come through them before. You can't—"

"This *crisis* of yours started a long while ago. If I remember, it was around 1927 that Muller first changed the genes in fruit flies with X-ray bombardment. That was the first step—over a hundred years before you was even born. Then came colchicine and the electron microscope and microsurgery, all in the next thirty years. But the day biological engineering really grew up—1962, Jenkins' and Scripture's gene charts and techniques—the Cities began to go. Little by little, people drifted out to the land again, raising the new crops, growing the new animals.

"The big Cities cannibalized the little ones, like an insect eating its own body when its food supply runs out. Now that's gone as far as it can, and you think it's just another crisis, but it isn't. It's the end."

Alvah heard a chill echo of Wytak's words: *"Rome fell. Babylon fell. The same thing can happen to New York..."*

He said, "What am I supposed to be, the rat that leaves the sinking ship?"

She sighed. "Alvah, you got a better brain than that. You don't *have* to think in metaphors or slogans, like a moron. I not asking you to join the winning side. That don't *matter*. In a few years there won't be but one side, no matter which way you jump."

"What do you want then?" he asked.

She looked dispirited. "Nothing, I guess. Let's go home."

It was a series of little things after that. There was the time he and Beej, out walking in the cool of the morning, stopped to rest at an isolated house that turned out to be occupied by George Allister of the Coffin clan, the shy little man who'd tried to show Alvah how to make his marks the day he landed.

George, Alvah believed—and questioning of Beej afterward confirmed it—was about as low on the social scale as a Muckfoot could get. But he was his own master. He had a wife and three children and neat fields, with his own animals grazing in them. His house was big and cool and clean. He poured them lemonade—which Alvah wistfully had to decline—from a sweating peacock-blue pitcher, while sitting at his ease on the broad front porch.

There were no servants among the Muckfeet. Alvah remembered an ancient fear of his, something that had cropped up in the old days every time he got seriously interested in a girl—that his children, if any, might relapse into the labor-pool category from which he had risen, or—it was hard to say which would be worse—into the servants' estate.

He went back from that outing very silent and thoughtful.

There was the time, a few days later, when Beej was working, and Alvah, at loose ends, wandered into a room in the laboratory building where two of Bither's assistants, girls he knew by sight, were sitting with two large, leathery-woody, pod-shaped boxes open on the bench between them.

Being hungry for company and preoccupied with himself at the same time, he didn't notice what should have been obvious, that the girls were busy at something private and personal. Even when they closed the boxes between them, he wasn't warned. "What's this?" he said cheerfully. "Can I see?"

They glanced at each other uncertainly. "These is our bride boxes," said the brunette. "We don't usual show them to singletons—"

They exchanged another glance.

"He's spoke for anyhow," said the redhead, with an enigmatic look at Alvah.

They opened the boxes. Inside each was a multitude of tiny compartments, each with a bit of something wrapped in cloth or paper tissue. The brunette chose one of the largest and unwrapped it with exaggerated care—an amorphous reddish-brown lump.

"Houseplant," she said, and wrapped it up again.

The redhead showed him a vial full of minuscule white spheres. "Weaver eggs. Two hundred of them. That's a lot, but I like more curtains and things than most."

"Wait a minute," said Alvah, perplexed. "What does a house-plant do?"

"Grow a house, of course," the brunette said. She held up another vial full of eggs. "Scavengers."

The redhead had a translucent sac with dark specks in it. "Utility trees."

"Garbage converter."

"This grow into a bed and these is chairbushes."

And so on, interminably, while the girls' eyes glittered and their cheeks flushed with enthusiasm.

The boxes, Alvah gathered, contained the germs of everything that would be needed to set up a Muckfoot household-beginning with the house itself. A thought struck him: "Does Beej have one of these outfits?"

Wide-eyed stares from both girls. "Well, of course!"

Alvah shifted uncomfortably. "Funny, she never mentioned it."

The girls exchanged another of those enigmatic glances and said nothing. Alvah, for some reason, grew more uncomfortable still. He tried once more. "What about the man—doesn't he have to put up anything?"

Yes, the man was expected to supply all the brutes and the seeds for outbuildings and all the crops except the bride's kitchen-garden. Everything in and around the home was her province, everything outside was his.

"Oh," said Alvah.

"But if a young fellow don't have all that through no fault of his own, his clan put up for him and let him pay back when he able."

"Ah," said Alvah and turned to make his escape.

The redhead called after him, "You thought any about what clan you like to get adopted into, Alvah?"

"Uh, no," said Alvah. "I don't think—"

"You talk to Doc Bither. He a elder of the Steins. Mighty good clan!"

Alvah bolted.

Then there was the Shakespeare business. It began in his third week in the Sticks, when he was already carrying a fleshy Muckfoot vegetable around with him—a radnip, B.J. called it. He hadn't had the nerve yet to bite into it, but he knew the time was coming when he would. Beej came to him and said, "Alvah, the Rinaldos' drama group is doing *Hamlet* next Saturday, and they short a Polonius. Do you think you could study it up by then?"

"What's Hamlet? And who's Polonius?"

She got the bird out of the library for him and he listened to the play, which turned out to be an archaic version of *The Manager of Copenhagen*. The text was nothing like the modernized abridgment he was used to, or the Muckfeet's slovenly speech either. It was full of words like *down-gyved* and *unkennel*. It was three-quarters incomprehensible until he began to get the hang of it, but it had a curious power. *For who would bear the whips and scorns of time, the oppressor's wrong, the proud man's contumely, the pangs of despised love,* and so on and so on. It rumbled, but it rumbled well.

Polonius, however, was the character Alvah knew as Paul Arnson, an inconsequential old man who only existed in the play to foul up the love affair between the principals and get killed in the third act. Alvah ventured to suggest that he might be of more use as Hamlet, but the director, a dry little man with a surprising boom to his voice, stubbornly insisted that all he needed was a Polonius—and seemed to intimate, without actually saying so that Alvah was a dim prospect even for that.

Alvah, with blood in his eye, accepted the part.

The rehearsals were a nightmare. The lines themselves gave him no trouble—Alvah was a quick study; in the realies, you had to be—and neither, at first, did the rustic crudity of the stage he was asked to perform on. Letter-perfect when the other actors were still stuttering and blowing their lines, he walked through the part with quiet competence and put the director's sour looks down to a witless hayseed hostility — until, three days before the performance, he suddenly awoke to the realization that everyone else in the cast was acting rings around him.

This wasn't the realies. There were no microphones to amplify his voice, no cameras to record every change in his expression. And the audience, what there was of it, was going to be *right — out — there.*

Alvah went to pieces. Trying to emulate the others' wide gestures and declamatory delivery only threw him further off his stride. He had never had stagefright in his life, but by curtain time on Saturday night, he was a pale and quivering wreck.

Dead and dragged off the stage at the end of act three, he got listlessly back into his own clothes and headed for an inconspicuous exit, but the director waylaid him. "Gustad," he said abruptly, "you ever thought of yourself as a professional actor?"

"I had some such idea at one time," Alvah said. "Why?"

"Well, I don't see why you shouldn't. If you work at it. I never see a man pick up so fast."

"What?" cried Alvah, thunderstruck.

"You wasn't bad," said the director. "A few rough edges, but a good performance. Now I happen to know some people in a few repertory companies — the Mondrillo Troupe, the Kalfoglou Repertory, one or two more. If you interested, I'll bird them and see if there's an opening. Don't thank me."

He moved off a few steps, then turned. "Oh, and, Gustad — get back into your costume, will you?"

"Uh," said Alvah. "But I'm dead. I mean—"

"For the curtain calls," said the director. "You don't want to miss those." He waved and walked back into the wings.

Alvah absently drew out his radnip and crunched off a bite of it. The taste was faintly unpleasant, like that of old protein paste or the wrong variety of culture-cheese, but he chewed and swallowed it.

That was when he realized that he had to get out. He didn't put on his costume again. Instead, he rummaged through the property boxes until he found an old pair of moleskin trousers and a stained squareweb shirt. He put them on, left by the rear door and headed south.

South for two reasons. First, because, he hoped, no one would look for him in that direction. Second, because he remembered what Beej had said that first day when they passed the display of tools: *"The metal comes from Iron Pits, just a few miles south of here."*

There might be some slender chance still that he could get the metal he needed, delouse the floater and go home in style — without the painful necessity of explaining to Wytak what had happened to the floater and all his goods and equipment. If not, he would simply keep on walking.

He had to do it now. He had almost waited too long as it was.

They had laid out the pattern of a life for him — to marry Beej, settle down in a house that would grow from a seed Beej kept in a pod-shaped box, be a rustic repertory actor, raise little Muckfeet. And the devil of it was, some unreasonable part of him wanted all of that!

A good thing he hadn't stayed for the curtain calls...

The Sun declined as he went, until he was walking down a ghost-dim road under the stars, with all the cool cricket-shrill world to himself.

He spent the night uncomfortably huddled under a hedge. Birds woke him with a great clamor in the tree-tops shortly after dawn. He washed himself and drank from a stream that crossed the fields, ate a purplish-red fruit he found growing nearby, then moved on.

Two hours later, he topped a ridge and found his way barred by a miles-long shallow depression in the Earth. Like the rest of the visible landscape, it was filled with an orderly checkerwork of growing plants.

There was nothing for it but to go through if he could. But surely he had gone more than "a few miles" by now?

The road slanted down the embankment to a gate in a high thorn hedge. Behind the gate was a kind of miniature domed kiosk and, in the kiosk, a sunburned man was dozing with a green-and-purple bird on his shoulder.

Alvah inspected a signboard that was entangled somehow in the hedge next to the gate. He was familiar enough by now with the Muckfeet's picture-writing to be fairly sure of what it said. The first symbol was a nail with an ax-head attached to it. That was *iron*. The second was a few stylized things that resembled fruit seeds. *Pits?*

He stared through the gate in mounting perplexity. You might call a place like this "Pits," all right but imagination boggled at calling it a mine. Still...

The kiosk, he noticed now, bore a scrawled symbol in orange pigment. He recognized that one, too; it was one of the common name-signs.

"Jerry!" he called.

"*Rrk,*" remarked the bird on the sleeping man's shoulder. "Kerry brogue; but the degradation of speech that occurs in London, Glasgow—"

"Oh, damn!" said Alvah. "You, there. *Jerry!*"

"*Rrk.* Kerry brogue; but the—"

"Jerry!"

"*Kerry brogue!*" shrieked the bird. The sunburned man sat up with a start and seized it by the beak, choking it off in the middle of "*degradation.*"

"Oh, hello," he said. "Don't know what it is about a Shaw bird, but they all alike. Can't shut them up."

"I'd like," said Alvah, "to look through the—uh—Pits. Would that be all right?"

"Sure," the man said cheerfully. He opened the gate and led the way down a long avenue between foot-high rows of plants.

"I Jerry Finch," he said. "Littleton clan. Don't believe you said your name."

"Harris," Alvah supplied at random. "I visiting from up north."

"Yukes?" the man inquired.

Alvah nodded, hoping for the best, and pointed at the plants they were passing. "What these?"

"Hinge blanks. Let them to forage last month. Won't have another crop here till August, and a poor one then. I telled Angus—he's the Pit boss—I telled him this soil's wore out, but he's a pincher—squeeze the last ton out and then go after the pounds and ounces. You should of saw what come off the ringbushes in the east hundred this April. Pitiful. Had to sell them for eyelets."

A cold feeling was running up Alvah's spine. He cleared his throat. "Got any knife blades?" he inquired with careful casualness.

"Mean bowies? Well, sure—right over yonder."

Alvah followed him to the end of the field and down three steps into the next. The plants here were much taller and darker, with stems thick and gnarled out of all proportion to their height. Here and there among the glossy leaves were incongruous glints of silvery steel.

Alvah stooped and peered into the foliage.

The silvery glints were perfectly formed six-inch chrome-steel knife blades. Each was attached to—*growing* from—the plant by way of a hard brown stem, exactly the right size and shape to serve as a handle.

He straightened carefully. "We do things a little different up north. You mind explaining briefly how the Pits works?"

Jerry looked surprised, but began readily enough. "These is like any other ferropositors. They extract the metal from the ores and deposit it in the bowie shape, or whatever it might be. Work from the outside in, of course, so you don't have no wood core to weaken it. We get a year's crops, average, before the ore used up. Then we bring the Earth-movers in, deepen the Pit a few feet, reseed and start over. Ain't much more to it."

Alvah stared at the fantastic growths. Well, why not? Plants that grew into knives or doorknobs or...

"What about alloys?" he asked.

"We got iron, lead and zinc. Carbon from the air. Other metals we got to import in granules. Like we get chrome from the Northwest Federation, mostly. They getting too big for their britches, though. Greedy. I think we going to switch over to you Yukes before long. Not that you fellows is any better, if you ask me, but at least—"

"Rhodium," said Alvah. "Palladium. What about them?"

"How's that?"

"Platinum group."

"Oh, sure, I know what you mean. We never use them. No call to. We could get you some, I guess—I think the Northwests got them. Take a few months, though."

"Suppose you wanted to make something out of a rhodopalladium alloy. How long would it take after you got the metals?"

"Well, you got to make a bush that would take and put them together, right proportions, right size, right shape. Depends. I guess if you was in a hurry—"

"Never mind," said Alvah wearily. "Thanks for the information." He turned and started back toward the gate.

When he was halfway there, he heard a hullabaloo break out somewhere behind him.

"Waw!" the voices seemed to be shouting. *"Waw! Waw!"*

He turned. A dozen paces behind him, Jerry and the bird on his shoulder were in identical neck-straining attitudes. Beyond them, on the near side of a group of low buildings three hundred yards away, three men were waving their arms madly and shouting, *"Waw! Waw!"*

"Wawnt to know what it is," the bird squawked. "I wawnt be a Mahn. Violet: you come along with me, to your own—"

"Shut up," said Jerry, then cupped his hands and yelled, "Angus, what is it?"

"Chicagos," the answer drifted back. "Just got word! They dusting Red Pits! Come *on!*"

Jerry darted a glance over his shoulder. "Come *on!*" he repeated and broke into a loping run toward the buildings.

Alvah hesitated an instant, then followed. With strenuous effort, he managed to catch up to the other man. "Where are we running to?" he panted. "Red Pits?"

"Don't talk foolish," Jerry gasped. "We running to shelter." He glanced back the way they had come. "Red Pits is over that way."

Alvah risked a look, and then another. The first time, he wasn't sure. The second time, the dusting of tiny particles over the horizon had grown to a cluster of visibly swelling black dots.

Other running figures were converging on the buildings as Alvah and Jerry approached. The dots were capsule shapes, perceptibly elongated, the size of a fingernail, a thumbnail, a thumb...

And under them on the land was a hurtling streak of golden haze, like dust stirred by a huge invisible finger.

Rounding the corner of the nearest building, Jerry popped through an open doorway. Alvah followed —

And was promptly seized from either side, long enough for something heavy and hard to hit him savagely on the nape of the neck.

VII

Bither was intent over a shallow vessel half full of a viscous clear liquid, with a great rounded veined-and-patterned glistening lump immersed in it, transparent in the phosphor-light that glowed from the sides of the container—a single living cell in mitosis, so grossly enlarged that every paired chromosome was visible. B.J. watched from the other side of the table, silent, breathing carefully, as the man's thick fingers dipped a hair-thin probe with minuscule precision, again and again, into the yeasty mass, excising a particle, splitting another, delicately shaving a third.

From time to time, she glanced at a sheet of horn intricately inscribed with numbers and genetic symbols. The chart was there for her benefit, not for Bither's—he never paused or faltered.

Finally, he sat back and covered the pan. "Turn on the lights and put that in the reduction fluid, will you, Beej? I bushed."

She whistled a clear note, and the dark globes fixed to the ceiling glowed to blue-white life. "You going to grow it right away?"

"Have to, I guess. Dammit, Beej, I hate making weapons."

"Not our choice. When you think it'll be?"

He shrugged. "War meeting this afternoon over at Council Flats. They'll let us know when it'll be."

She was silent until she had transferred the living lump from one container to another and put it away. Then, "Hear anything more?"

"They dusting every ore-bed from here to the Illinois, looks like. Crystal, Butler's—"

"*Butler's!* That's worked out."

"I know it. We let them land there. They'll find out." After another pause, Bither said, "No word about Alvah, Beej. I sorry."

She nodded. "Wouldn't be, this early."

He looked at her curiously. "You still think he'll be back?"

"If the dust ain't got him. Lay you odds."

"Well," said Bither, lifting the cover of another pan to peer into it, "I hope you—"

"Ozark Lake nine-one-two-five," said a reedy voice from the corner. "Ozark Lake nine—"

"Get that, will you, Beej?"

B.J. picked up the ocher spheroid from its shelf and said into its tympanum, "Bither Laboratories."

"This Angus Littleton at Iron Pits," the thing said. "Let me talk to Bither."

She passed it over, holding a loop of its rubbery cord — the beginning of a miles-long sheathed bundle of cultivated neurons that linked it, via a "switchboard" organism, with thousands like it in this area alone, and with millions more across the continent.

"This Doc Bither. What is it, Angus?"

"Something funny for you, Doc. We got a couple prisoners here, one a floater pilot, other a Chicago spy."

"Well, what you want me to—"

"*Wait,* can't you? This spy claim he know you, Doc. Say his name's Custard. Alvah Custard."

Alvah stared out through the window, puzzled and angry. He had been in the room for about half an hour, while things were going on outside. He had tried to break the window. The pane had bent slightly. It was neither glass nor plastic, and it wasn't breakable.

Outside, the last of the invading floaters was dipping down toward the horizon, pursued by a small darting black shape. Golden-dun haze obscured all the foreground except the first few rows of plants, which were drooping on their stems. The squadron had made one grand circle of the mine area, dusting as they went, before the Muckfeet on their incredibly swift flyers—birds or reptiles, Alvah couldn't tell which—had risen to engage them. Since then, a light breeze from the north had carried the stuff dropped over the Pits: radioactive dust with a gravitostatic charge to make it rebound and spread—and then, with its polarity reversed, cling like grim death where it fell.

He turned and looked at the other man, sitting blank-faced and inattentive, wearing a rumpled sky-blue uniform, on the bench against the inner wall. Most of the squadron had flown off to the west after that first pass, and had either escaped or been forced down somewhere beyond the Pits. This fellow had crash-landed in the fields not five hundred yards from Alvah's window. Alvah had seen the Muckfeet walking out to the wreck—strolling fantastically through the deadly haze—and turkey-trotting their prisoner back again. A little later, someone had opened the door and shoved the man in, and there he had sat ever since.

His skin-color was all right. He was breathing evenly and seemed in no discomfort. As far as Alvah could see, there was not a speck of the death-dust anywhere on his skin, hair or clothing. But mad as it was, this was not the most incongruous thing about him.

His uniform was of a cut and pattern that Alvah had seen only in pictures. There was a C on each gleaming button and, on the bar of the epaulette, Chicagoland. In short, he was evidently a Floater Force officer from Chicago. The only trouble was that Alvah recognized him. He was a grips by day at the Seven Boroughs studios, famous for his dirty jokes, which he acquired at his night job in the Under Queens Power Station. He was a lieutenant j.g. in the N.Y. F.F. Reserve, and his name was Joe *"Dimples"* Mundry.

Alvah went over and sat down beside him again. Mundry's normally jovial face was set in wooden lines. His eyes focused on Alvah, but without recognition.

"Joe—"

"My name," said Mundry obstinately, "is Bertram Palmer, Float Lieutenant, Windy City Regulars. My serial number is 79016935."

That was the only tune he knew. Alvah hadn't been able to get another word out of him. Name, rank and serial number—that was normal. Members of the armed services were naturally conditioned to say nothing else if captured. But why throw in the name of his outfit?

One, that was the way they did things in Chicago, and there just happened to be a Chicago soldier who looked and talked exactly like Joe Mundry, who had the same scars on his knuckles from brawls with the generator monkeys. Two, Alvah's mind had snapped. Three, this was a ringer foisted on Alvah for some incomprehensible purpose by the Muckfeet. And four—a wild and terrible suspicion...

Alvah tried again. "Listen, Joe, I'm your friend. We're on the same side. *I'm not a Muckfoot.*"

"My name is Bertram Palmer, Float Lieutenant—"

"Joe, I'm leveling with you. Listen—remember the Music Hall story, the one about the man who could..." Alvah explained in detail what the man could do. It was obscenely improbable and very funny, if you liked that sort of thing, and it was a story Joe had told him two days before he left New York.

A gleam of intelligence came into Joe's eyes. "What's the punch-line?" he demanded.

"'What the hell did you want to change the key on me for?'" Alvah replied promptly.

Joe looked at him speculatively. "That might be an old joke. Maybe they even know it in the Sticks. And my name isn't Joe."

He really believed he was Bertram Palmer of the Windy City Regulars, that much seemed clear. Also, if it was possible that the Muckfeet knew that story, it was likelier still that the Chicagolanders knew it.

"All right," said Alvah, "ask me a question—something I couldn't know if I were a Muckfoot. Go ahead, anything. A place, or something that happened recently, or whatever you want."

A visible struggle was going on behind Joe's face. "Can't think of anything," he said at last. "Funny."

Alvah had been watching him closely. "Let's try this. Did you see *Manhattan Morons?*"

Joe looked blank. "What?"

"The realie. You mean you missed it? *Manhattan Morons?* Till I saw that, I never really knew what a comical bunch of weak-minded, slobber-mouthed, monkey-faced drooling idiots those New Yorkers—"

Joe's expression had not changed, but a dull red flush had crept up over his collar. He made an inarticulate sound and lunged for Alvah's throat.

When Angus Littleton opened the door, with Jerry and B.J. behind him, the two men were rolling on the floor.

"What made you think he was a spy?" B.J. demanded. They were a tight, self-conscious group in the corridor. Alvah was nursing a split lip.

"Said he was a Yuke," Jerry offered, "but didn't seem too sure, so I said the Yukes was greedy. He never turned a hair. And he acted like he never saw a mine before. Things like that."

B.J. nodded. "It was a natural mistake, I guess. Well, thanks for calling us, Angus."

"Easy," said Angus, looking glum. "We ain't out of the rough yet, Beej."

"What do you mean? He didn't have anything to do with this attack—he's from New York."

"He *say* he is, but how you know? What make you think he ain't from Chicago?"

Alvah said, "While you're asking that, you might ask another question about him." He jerked a thumb toward the closed door. "What makes you think *he* is?"

The other three stared at him thoughtfully. "Alvah," Beej began, "what you aiming at? Do you think—"

"I'm not sure," Alvah interrupted. "I mean I'm sure, but I'm not sure I want to tell you. Look," he said, turning to Angus, "let me talk to her alone for a few minutes, will you?"

Angus hesitated, then walked away down the hall, followed by Jerry.

"You've got to explain some things to me about this raid," said Alvah when they were out of hearing. "I *saw* those floaters dusting and it was the real thing. I can tell by the way the plants withered. But your people were walking around out there. Him, too—the prisoner. How come?"

"Antirads," said the girl. "Little para-insects, like the metallo-phage—the metallophage was developed from them. When you been exposed, the antirads pick the dust particles off you and de-posit them in radproof pots. They die in the pots, too, and we bury the whole—"

"All right," Alvah said. "How long have you had those things? Is there any chance the Cities knew about it?"

"The antirads was developed toward the end of the last City war. That was what ended it. First we stopped the bombing, and then when they used dust—You never heard of any of this?"

"No," Alvah told her. "Third question, what are you going to do about Chicago now, on account of this raid?"

"Pull it down around their ears," B.J. said gravely. "We never did before partly because it wasn't necessary. We knowed for the last thirty years that the Cities could never be more than a nuisance to us again. But this isn't just a raid. They've attacked us all over the district—ruined the crops in every mine. We must put an end to it now—not that it make much difference, this year or ten years from now. And it isn't as if we couldn't save the people..."

"Never mind that," said Alvah abstractedly. Then her last words penetrated. "No, go ahead—what?"

"I started to say, we think we'll be able to save the people, thanks to what we learned from you. It's just Chicago we going to destroy, not the—"

"Learned from *me?*" Alvah repeated. "What do you mean?"

"We learned that, when it's a question of survival, a City man can overcome his conditioning. You proved that. Did you eat the radnip?"

"Yes."

"There, you see? And you'll eat another and, sooner or later, you'll realize they taste good. A human being can learn to like anything that's needful to him. We're adaptable—you can't condition that out of us without breaking us."

Alvah stared at her. "But you spent over two weeks on me. How you going to do that with fifteen or twenty million people all at once?"

"We can do it. You was the pilot model—two weeks for you. But now that we know how, we pretty sure we can do it in three days— the important part, getting them to eat the food. And it's a good thing the storehouses is full, all over this continent."

They looked at each other silently for a moment. "But the Cities has to go," B.J. said.

"Fourth and last question," he said. "If a City knew about your radiation defenses all along, what would be their reason for attacking you this way?"

"Our first idea was that it was just plain desperation—they had to do something and there wasn't anything they could do that would work, so they just did something that wouldn't. Or maybe they hoped they'd be able to hold the mines long enough to get some metal out, even though they knew it was foolish to hope."

"That was your first idea. What was your second?"

She hesitated. "You remember what I told you, that the Cities cannibalized each other for a while, the big ones draining population away from the little ones and reclaiming their metals—and you remember I said that had gone as far as it could?"

"Yes."

"Well, when the big fish have eat up all the little fish they can eat each other till there's just one big fish left."

"And?" asked Alvah tensely.

"And maybe one City might think that, if they got us to make war on another, they could step in when the fighting was over and get all the metals they'd need to keep them going for years. So they might send raiding parties out in the other City's uniforms, and condition them to think they really were from that City. Was that what happened, Alvah?"

Alvah nodded reluctantly. "I don't understand it. They must have started planning this as soon as I stopped communicating. It doesn't make sense. They couldn't be that desperate—or maybe they could. Anyway, it's a dirty stunt. It isn't like New York."

She said nothing—too polite to contradict him, Alvah supposed.

Down at the end of the hall, Angus was beginning to look impatient. Alvah said, "So now you'll pull New York down?"

"Alvah, it may sound funny, but I think you know this, really—you really doing your people a favor."

"If that's so," he said wryly, "then New York was 'really' trying to do one for Chicago."

"I was hoping you'd see that it doesn't matter. It might have been Chicago that went first, or Denver, or any of the others, but that isn't important—they all have to go. What's important is the people. This may be another thing that's hard for you to accept, but they going to be happier, most of them."

And maybe she was right, Alvah thought, if you counted in everybody, labor pool, porters and all. Why shouldn't you count them, he asked himself defiantly—they were people, weren't they? Maybe the index of civilization was not only how much you had, but how hard you had to work for it—incessantly, like the New Yorkers, holding down two or three jobs at once, because the City's demands were endless—or, like the Muckfeet, judiciously and with honest pleasure.

"Alvah?" said the girl. She put her question no more explicitly than that, but he knew what she meant.

"Yes, Beej," replied Alvah Gustad, Muckfoot.

VIII

On the Jersey flats, hidden by a forest of traveler trees, a sprawling settlement took form—mile after mile of forced-growth dwellings, stables, administration buildings, instruction centers. It was one of five. There was another farther north in Jersey, two in the Poconos and one in the vestigial state of Connecticut.

They lay empty, waiting, their roofs sprouting foliage that perfectly counterfeited the surrounding forests. Roads had been cleared, converging toward the City, ending just short of the half-mile strip of wasteland that girdled New York, and it was there that Alvah stood.

He found it strange to feel himself ready to walk unprotected across that stretch of country, knowing it to be acrawl with tiny organisms that had been developed not to tolerate Man's artificial buildings, whether of stone, metal, cement or plastics, but crumbled them all to the ground. Stranger still to be able to visualize the crawling organisms without horror or disgust.

But the strangest of all was to be looking at the City from this viewpoint. The towers stared back at him across the surrounding wall, tall and shining and proud, the proudest human creation—a century ago. Pitifully outdated today, the gleaming Cities fought back, unaware that they had lost long ago, that their bright spires and elaborate gadgets were as antiquated as polished armor would have been against a dun-painted motorized army.

"I wish I could go with you," said Beej from the breathing forest at his back.

"You can't," Alvah replied without turning. "They wouldn't let you through the gate alive. They know me, but even so, I'm not sure they'll let me in after all this time. Have to wait and see."

"You know you don't have to go. I mean—"

"I know what you mean," said Alvah unhappily, "and you're right. But all the same, I do have to go. Look Beej, you've got that map I drew. It's a ten-to-one chance that, if I don't make the grade, they'll put me in the quarantine cells right inside the wall. So you're not to worry. Okay?"

"Okay," she promised, worried.

He kissed her and watched her fade back into the forest where the others were—Bither and Artie Brumbacher and a few others from home, the rest Jerseys and other clansmen from the Seaboard Federation—cheerful, matter-of-fact people who were going to bear most of the burden of what was coming, and never tired of reminding the inlanders of the fact.

He turned and walked out across the wasteland, crunching the dry weeds under his feet.

There was a flaming moat around the City and, beyond the moat, high in the wall, a closed gateway—corroded tight, probably; it was a very long time since the City had had any traffic except by air. But there was a spy tower above the gate. Alvah walked up directly opposite its bulbous idiot eyes, waved, and then waited.

After a long time, an inconspicuous port in the tower squealed open and a fist-sized dark ovoid darted out across the flames. It came to rest in midair, two yards from Alvah. It clicked and said crisply, "State your name and business."

"Alvah Gustad. I just got back from a confidential mission for the City Manager. Floater broke down, communicator, everything. I had to walk back. Tell him I'm here."

The ovoid hovered exactly where it was, as if pinned against the air. Alvah waited. When he got tired of standing, he dropped his improvised knapsack on the ground and sat on it. Finally the ovoid said harshly, in another voice, "Who are you and what do you want?"

Alvah patiently gave the same answer.

"What do you mean, broke down?"

"Broke *down*," said Alvah. "Wouldn't run any more."

Silence. He settled himself for another long wait, but it was only five minutes or thereabouts before the ovoid said, "Strip."

When he had done so, the gate opposite broke open with a scream of tortured metal and ground itself back into a recess in the wall. The drawbridge, a long rust-pitted tongue of metal, thrust out and down to span the moat, a wall of flame on either side of it.

Alvah walked across nimbly, the metal already hot against his naked soles, and the drawbridge whipped back into its socket. The gate screamed shut.

The room was the same, the anthems were the same. Alvah, disinfected, shaved all over and clad in an airtight glassine overall with its own air supply, stopped short two paces inside the door. The man behind the Manager's desk was not Wytak. It was jowly, red-faced Ellery McArdle, Commissioner of the Department of War.

One of the guards prodded Alvah and he kept going up to the desk. "Now I think I get it," he said, staring at McArdle. "When—"

McArdle's cold gaze flickered. Then his heavy head dropped forward a trifle, and he said, "Finish what you were saying, Gustad."

"I was about to remark," Alvah said, "that when Wytak's pet project flopped, he lost enough support to let you impeach him. Is that right?"

McArdle nodded and seemed to lose interest. "Your feet are not swollen or blistered, Gustad. You didn't walk back from the Plains. How did you get here?"

Alvah took a deep breath. "We flew—on a passenger roc—as far as the Adirondacks. We didn't want to alarm you by too much air traffic so near the City, so we joined a freight caravan there."

McArdle's stony face did not alter, but all the meaning went suddenly out of it. It was as if the man himself had stepped back and shut a door. The porter behind his chair swayed and looked as if he were about to faint. Alvah heard one of the guards draw in his breath sharply.

"*Fthuh!*" said McArdle abruptly, his face contorting. "Let's get this over. What do you know about the military plans of the Muck-feet? Answer me fully. If I'm not satisfied that you do, I'll have you worked over till I am satisfied."

Alvah, who had been feeling something like St. George and something like a plucked chicken, discovered that anger could be a very comforting thing. "That's what I came here to do," he said tightly. "The Muckfeets' military plans are about what you might have expected, after that lousy trick of yours. They know it wasn't Chicago that raided them."

McArdle started and made as if to rise. Then he sank back, staring fixedly at Alvah.

"They've had a gutful. They're going to finish New York."

"When?" said McArdle, biting the word off short.

"That depends on you. If you're willing to be reasonable, they'll wait long enough for you to dicker with them. Otherwise, if I'm not back in about an hour, the fun starts."

McArdle touched a stud, said, "Green alert," pressed the stud again and laced his fingers together on the desk. "Hurry it up," he said to Alvah. "Let's have the rest."

"I'm going to ask you to do something difficult," said Alvah. "It's this—think about what I'm telling you. You're not thinking now, you're just reacting—"

He heard a slight movement behind him, saw McArdle's eyes flicker and his hand make a *Not now* gesture.

"You're in the same room with a man who's turned Muckfoot and it disgusts you. You'll be cured of that eventually—you can be, I'm the proof—but all I want you to do now is put it aside and use your brains. Here are the facts. Your raiding parties got the shorts beat off them. I saw one of the fights—it lasted about twenty minutes. The Muckfeet could have polished off the Cities any time in the last thirty years. They haven't done it till now, because—"

McArdle was beating time with his fingertips on the polished ebonite. He wasn't really listening, Alvah saw, but there was nothing for it except to go ahead.

"—they had the problem of deconditioning and re-educating more than twenty million innocent people, or else letting them starve to death. Now they have the knowledge they need. They can—"

"The terms," said McArdle.

"They're going to close down this—this reservation," Alvah said. "They'll satisfy you in any way you like that they can do it by force. If you help, it can be an orderly process in which nobody gets hurt and everybody gets the best possible break. And they'll keep the City intact as a museum. I talked them into that. Or, if they have to, they'll take the place apart slab by slab."

McArdle's mouth was working violently. "Take him out and kill him, for City's sake! And, Morgan!" he called when Alvah and his guards were halfway to the door.

"Yes, Mr. Manager."

"When you're through, paint him green and dump him out the gate he came in."

It was a pity about Wytak, Alvah's brain was telling him frozenly. Wytak was a scoundrel or he could never have got where he was—had been—but he wasn't afraid of a new idea. It might have been possible to deal with Wytak.

"Where we going to do it?" the younger one asked nervously. He had been pale and sweating in the floater all the way across Middle Jersey.

"In the disinfecting chamber," Morgan said, gesturing with his pistol. "Then we haul him straight out. In there, you."

"Well, let's get it over with," the younger one said. "I'm sick."

"You think *I'm* not sick?" said Morgan in a strained voice. He gave Alvah a final shove into the middle of the room and stood back, adjusting his gun.

Alvah found himself saying calmly, "Not that way, Morgan, unless you want to turn black and shrivel up a second after."

"What's he talking about?" the boy whispered shakily

"Nothing," said Morgan. The hand with the gun moved indecisively.

"To puncture me," Alvah warned, "you've got to puncture the suit. And I've been eating Muckfeet food for the last month and a half. I'm full of micro-organisms—swarming with them. They'll bloop out of me straight at *you,* Morgan."

Both men jerked back, as if they had been stung. "I'm getting outa here!" said the boy, grabbing for the door stud.

Morgan blocked him. "Stay here!"

"What're you going to do?" the younger one asked.

He swore briefly. "We'll tell the O. D. Come on."

The door closed and locked solidly behind them. Alvah looked to see if there was a way to double-lock it from his side, but there wasn't. He tried the opposite door to make sure it was locked, which it was. Then he examined the disinfectant nozzles, wondering if they could be used to squirt corrosive in on him. He decided they probably couldn't and, anyhow, he had no way to spike the nozzles. Then there was nothing to do but sit in the middle of the bare room and wait, which he did.

The next thing that happened was that he heard a faint far-off continuous noise through the almost soundproof door. He stood up and went over and put his ear against the door, and decided it was his imagination.

Then there was a noise, and he jumped back, his skin tingling all over, just before the door slid open. The sudden maniacal clangor of a bell swept Morgan into the room with it, wild-eyed, his cap missing, drooling from a corner of his mouth, his gun high in one white-knuckled fist with the muzzle, big as a cannon pointing straight at Alvah.

"*Glah!*" said Morgan, and pulled the trigger.

Alvah's heart went *bonk* hard against his ribs, and the room blurred. Then he realized that there hadn't been any hiss of an ejected pellet. And he was still on his feet. And Morgan, with his mouth stretched open all the way back to the uvula, was standing there a yard away, staring at him and pulling the trigger repeatedly.

Alvah stepped forward half a pace and put a straight left squarely on the point of Morgan's jaw. As the man fell, there were shrieks and running footsteps in the outer room. Somebody in Guard uniform plunged past the doorway, shouting incoherently, caromed off a wall, dwindled down a corridor. Then the room was full of leaping men in motley.

The first of them was Artie Brumbacher, almost unrecognizable because he was grinning from ear to ear. He handed Alvah a four-foot knobkerrie and a bulging skin bag and said, "Let's go!"

Alvah looped the bag's strap hurriedly over his shoulder. The bag seemed to be full of something brown and heavily mushy, about the consistency of wet sand. There were spatters of what looked like the same stuff on the walls and floor of the outer corridor; otherwise the place was empty. There was nobody behind the guard desk in the lobby, and the riot guns were still racked neatly in their case. "Artie, what's this?" he asked as they went. "Didn't you bring any dogs? How'd you get past the guards, anyhow?"

"Didn't need no dogs," said Artie, his eyes roving. "This here did the business." He patted the bag he carried. "Idea of Doc's—he fixed it up at the last minute, and it sure does work. Show you later."

Then they were out in the open, and Alvah had no time for further questions. Half a dozen rocs were circling overhead; except for them, the air was empty.

Alvah paused to try to open the zippers of his glassine coverall; they were sealed tight. After a minute Artie saw his trouble, and sliced off the hood of the coverall with two casual strokes of his bowie. "Come on," he said again.

The streets were full of grounded floaters and stalled surface cars. The bells had fallen silent, and so had the faint omnipresent vibration that was like silence itself until it was gone. Not a motor was turning in the Borough of Jersey. Occasional chittering sounds floated on the air, and muffled buzzings and other odd sounds, all against the background chorus of faraway shrieks that rose and fell.

At the corner of Middle Orange and Weehawken, opposite the Superior Court Building, they came upon a squad of Regulars who had thrown away their useless guns and picked up an odd lot of assorted bludgeons—lengths of pipe, tripods and the like.

"Now you'll see," said Artie.

The Regulars set up a ragged yell and came running forward. The two Muckfeet on either side of Alvah, Artie and the buck-toothed one called Lafe, dipped heaping dark-brown handfuls out of the bags they carried slung from their shoulders. Alvah followed suit, and recognized the stuff at last—bran meal, soaked in some fragrant syrup until it was mucilaginous and heavy.

Artie swung first, then Lafe, and Alvah last—and the soggy lumps smacked the foremost faces. The squad broke, wiping frenziedly. But you couldn't wipe the stuff off. It clung coldly and grainily to the hair on the backs of your hands and your eyelashes and the nap of your clothing. All you could do was move it around.

One berserker with a smeared face didn't stop, and Lafe dropped him with a knobkerrie between the eyes. One more, a white-faced youth, stood miraculously untouched, still hefting his club. He took a stride forward menacingly.

Grinning, Artie raised another glob of the mash and ate it, smacking his lips. The youth spun around, walked drunkenly to the nearest wall and was rackingly sick.

Charles Fairweather was a realie actor, a concupiscent little man with a soft paunch and a gray close-clipped mustache. His rimless glasses softened the wicked gleam in his eye; he looked the very image of a pompous, ineffectual little executive. He was often cast as the bewildered father in a domestic comedy, and in fact had enjoyed a long run some ten years ago in the best-rated domestic series of them all, *Dangerous Dolores.* He had a talent for high comedy which he seldom got a chance to use; but his services were in demand, he ate regularly and enjoyed himself. He had been married and divorced twice; at present he was a bachelor. He liked the girls, and to tell the truth, the girls liked him.

This week he was in rehearsal for a special, a ninety-minute Western about an Old Los Angeles veterinarian and his struggles against Peke-poisoners. Alvah Gustad had been penciled in for the lead, but at the last minute some conflict had developed, and Buddy Riggs had been signed. Fairweather played a minor role, the choleric police chief; his contribution consisted mainly of waving a cigar and banging his desk.

It wasn't a bad show. They had two real dogs from the Bronnix Zoo, nasty orange bits of business, and the girl who played the nurse was a new face, a cute brunette, not more than eighteen, with a cleavage that bulged nicely in her low-cut uniform. Fairweather was watching her, stroking his mustache, as she rehearsed a scene where she had to lean over a sick Peke. The beast, groggy from dope, rolled its yellow eyes up at her and weakly bared a fang. The cleavage was toothsome.

There was a sudden gold-dust glitter in the air, too swift to be clearly seen. Fairweather blinked, and rubbed his eyes under the rimless glasses. His eyes were tired; he'd been out late the night before.

Number two camera, which was suspended in its floater field facing the actress, slowly began to sink. The nearby monitor shifted from the actress's face to the same view Fairweather was enjoying, then without pausing lowered still more to pick up the Peke. It kept going, to an angle shot of the operating table, and then a blurred closeup of the floor.

"Hey!" somebody shouted over the intercom. Fairweather looked around, with a prickling of uneasiness up the back of his neck. All over the set, cameras were drifting downward at the same rate. They bobbed slightly as their fields touched the floor, then went on sinking, a little more slowly, until the gray-painted ovoids were actually resting on the hard plastic. The monitor screens showed crazy angles and blurs.

A shout of profanity came out of the intercom. "I'll get on it, Burt," another voice called. Jack Drew, the chief technician, came hurrying down out of the booth. Electricians and grips were converging on the working panels, over behind the set. The actress looked up uncertainly, then moved a little away from the Peke and signaled her porter for a cigarette. Fairweather stayed where he was, feeling decidedly uneasy.

He glanced around, and saw the rest of the actors and crew standing in similar puzzled attitudes. They all felt it. But there was nothing to be seen. Even the faint golden blurring of the air that he had noticed before was gone. Nothing on the floor of the studio, nothing behind the sets, nothing—He peered up at the ceiling. Up there, among the spidery suspended arms of the scene-moving machinery, something long and threadlike and green was swaying... lengthening, coming nearer. Fairweather stared at it. Then he saw another. And another.

They were hanging from the ceiling in faintly visible festoons— threads of green with something indefinably unpleasant about them. The ceiling seemed covered with them now, and there were more dangling threads all the time.

Something made a small sound at Fairweather's feet, and he looked down to see a hand-sized splash of sticky green on the plastic. Off at the other end of the stage, somebody yelled.

There was another small sound, a *pot,* and then another, and two together. Fairweather saw a fat drop detach itself from one of the threads and start to fall. The things were *dripping.*

Somebody started to ran. Fairweather caught a glimpse of Ernie Rillup, the music director, wiping frantically at his green-smeared face. Then more people were running. The brunette actress threw her cigarette away, white-faced, and started after them.

"Muckfeet!" shouted somebody, and abruptly the faint reek in the air grew nauseously strong.

Plop, went a larger, greener drop.

Then they were all running.

Artie's squad was picking its way among the piled hulks of floaters grounded on Upper Holland Boulevard. Most of the craft were taxis and civilian scoots, but there was a shiny military floater every now and then. They had to go slowly, both because the disabled machines were so close together, and because they wanted to make sure no military personnel were hiding in the clutter.

There was a sudden flapping noise. Alvah looked up, and saw a flock of small gray birds come fluttering down to rest on the shoulders of the Muckfeet. They were gray-feathered parrots with big, brainy-looking heads. The nearest one, alighting on Artie, said, "*Rrrrk.* Browns to Greens. We having trouble at the Fulton Street Armory. Send us some help. *Rrk.*" Up and down the line, the other parrots were saying the same thing, in a ragged bird chorus.

"Okay," Artie said. "Green squad nine to Browns. Go on back and tell 'em we coming." The parrot squawked and took off in a flurry of feathers. After a moment the other birds flew up, too. The main flock wheeled and then headed off to the northwest; Artie's parrot flew eastward by itself.

"Fulton Street," Artie was saying, as he unfolded an onionskin map. "You know where that is, Alvah?"

"Sure I do. But it's a long way over on foot," Alvah said. "Hadn't we better get some transportation?"

"Might as well," Artie told him, and put a brown whistle pod to his lips. No sound came out, though his cheeks bulged. He put the whistle away. "Show me where this place is at, will you?" he asked, spreading out the map. "Lessee, we here now..."

Alvah, somewhat perplexed, located the Armory in the tracery of gray lines and pointed to it. "Our best route is probably across the LaGuardia Overpass, then down the Hudson River Floatway," he began, but Artie shook his head.

"No, nev' mind that. Look yonder."

Between the skyline and the Roof, half a dozen massive gray shapes were flapping slowly along. The huge wings moved so slowly, they seemed to be merely rowing the air; but while he watched, they grew rapidly larger. In a few moments they were stalling to land, and the buffeting of their huge wings made the men stagger. They came down hard, their big bodies thumping where they landed atop the stalled floaters. They were rocs, gigantic lizard-gray creatures with reptilian heads and fierce yellow eyes. They were plumed and pinioned like birds; only along the skull the feathers gave way to short gray spines.

"Come on," said Artie. The other members of the squad were already scrambling over the piled floater bodies, climbing astride the rocs behind the helmeted riders.

Alvah followed without pleasure; he had already had one roc ride, and had considered it sufficient. The Muckfeet were piling up happily in rows, five or six to a bird, each hanging onto the man ahead of him, with their legs dangling over the roc's narrow gray sides. Artie motioned Alvah up ahead of him and got on behind. Gripping and being gripped, Alvah held his breath and waited for the takeoff.

At a command from the rider up ahead, the huge bird spread its wings. Flapping thunderously, it started forward along the line of floaters; Alvah could hear the big gray talons scraping and scrabbling at the metal. He held on desperately. With a lurch, they were airborne. The boulevard dropped away below; the dim translucent rectangles of the Roof drew nearer.

From the air, as they approached, they could see something was going on around the black oval bulk of the Armory. For two blocks around, the streets were empty, and near the building itself, there was a mound of smoking wreckage of some kind. The roc glided down, and Alvah lost sight of the Armory as they landed behind a building three blocks away.

Feeling dizzy, he got down from the beast's back and followed Artie over to a little knot of excited Muckfeet.

"—wish we'd of brought the dogs," somebody was saying stridently.

"Well, you know what we decided," a square brown man said impatiently. He had a group commander's patch on his tunic; he was a Jersey named Korner, whom Alvah knew slightly. He went on, "Dogs would of attacked civilians, and we didn't want that. We could still bring 'em in on leash, but that would take about half an hour, and by that time—"

"What's going on anyhow?" Artie interrupted plaintively. "Bird said you run into trouble. Where's it at?"

Korner gestured toward the Armory. "Some Newyorks holed up in there and started to heave explosives out the top windows. We sent in airweed and that, but it didn't get them out. We getting ready to soften the doors when they beat us to it, come out running with some kind of suits on—hoods, dinguses to breathe through and that. Must be two hundred. We trying to keep them bottled up, but this stinking place got about a million underground corridors. That why we got to have more men. Otherwise before we catch them all, they going to spread out all over the city and make more trouble than you can spit."

Artie whistled. "What kind of weapons they got?"

"Mostly clubs, but some got axes and that. Some got homemade bombs, and they all crazy mad. They don't care if they get killed, just so they kill you, so look out. They got Ernie Pierce and two other good boys."

Artie hefted his knobkerrie. "All right. What you want us to do?"

"You and your squad spread out that way. Try to keep 'em from getting any farther west. I'll give you a couple message birds. You need any help, I'll try to send it, but we awful thin as it is."

Korner turned away, to meet another group that was just arriving. Artie nodded to his men. "All right, let's go."

Half an hour after leaving the rest of the squad, the five of them were moving cautiously along a substreet arcade when there was a sudden scuffling of feet, and a half-dozen leaping figures charged them from the side. Alvah caught a startled glimpse of inhuman faces and stocky blue bodies. One of the Muckfeet was down, sprawled on the corridor floor. The others were fanning out, defending themselves with knobkerries. The corridor echoed to the sound of their whacks.

Alvah found himself working hard to fend off one masked, muffled figure that was trying its best to split his skull with a steel bar. The eyes stared wildly through round goggles; the rest of the face was grotesque in a respirator. The man's body was completely covered in heavy blue cloth, including hands and feet. It must be hot and cramped in that suit, but Alvah, in the freedom of borrowed Muckfoot clothing, still found he had all he could do to hold his own. The masked man's steel bar grazed his ear and left his skull ringing. He staggered, caught his balance with a desperate effort, and fought back.

The scuffling group drifted into a new pattern. Alvah gulped air, surged forward with knobkerrie swinging mightily, and forced his opponent to give ground until he was back to back with another blue figure. At the contact, the two sprang away from each other; Alvah's man looked over his shoulder, and Alvah seized the opportunity to whang him on the head. He dropped, and Alvah joined forces with another Muckfoot to topple the second man.

Breathing hard, they stopped to survey the damage. Two of the five Muckfeet were down, one groaning and hugging himself, the other motionless. The half-dozen Newyorks were all stretched out in various attitudes. Artie, dripping gore from a split cheek, ordered them stripped and relieved of their weapons. He broke a capsule of airweed spores and smeared the gel on one of the corridor walls. In twenty minutes or so the fast-growing stuff would begin to climb over the ceiling, adding to its slimy bulk by absorbing moisture from the air. When the Newyorks came to, any of them that could walk would go out into the street to get away from the airweed. The rest could be picked up by hospital details later. The stunned Muckfoot was left where he was for the time being, and the other injured man was helped back to the Armory site by another Muckfoot. That left Artie and Alvah; they moved on.

Rage and fear walked with Major Walt Reardon in the heavy suit. He could smell it in his own confined stink; he was sweating all over, and the evaporator on the back of the suit wasn't helping. These were emergency suits, never meant for long and continuous use. But they were better than surrender.

He swung his club wearily at the threads of green that dripped from the corridor ceiling. They broke and spattered, like the bodies of enemies, but it was distant and unreal. All that was outside—glove, club, green tendrils. He was inside, and he couldn't get out.

His breath made a hoarse sucking noise in the respirator close to his mouth. It was a good respirator, he knew he couldn't be suffering from lack of air, but it felt that way. The suit touched him clammily all around as he moved. Not for an instant could he forget it was there.

Tears stung his eyes when he remembered the bright NYFF floaters falling out of the air—drifting down, without a shot fired, defeated. If they'd only had a chance to fight!

Spread out, that was the thing. The bastards were thick as flies around the Armory. They had jumped him in the Centre Street Concourse, split his detail; he had got away through the deserted public baths, but heaven only knew what had happened to Yingling and Garrison and the rest. Spread out, that was the order. He had stayed underground, in spite of the green mess—while the damned Muckfeet strutted around up there—and he'd stay under until he was ready to come up. Catch them by surprise; kill.

"Can't do that to *us*," he said hoarsely.

Bright visions of Muckfeet with split skulls shimmered in his head. He peered around them, trying to see the street signs at the corridor intersection ahead. They were overgrown with green fuzzy threads, like the rest, unreadable. Even the light-emitting walls were beginning to glow greenish through the tendrils; it was like being under water.

He crossed the corridor, wavering, and scrubbed the slime off a display window. Inside, dimly visible through the green film, were half a dozen realie packets. He could see the languorous girls on the covers, and read some of the titles: "MEET ME IN CANARSIE, with Lew Rock and Ella Lorn"; "I LOVE YOU THURSDAY, with the New Sensation, Tommy-Ann Welle." Yes, that was the window; he had passed it a hundred times. He knew where he was now; it was time to come up. He turned right, following the cross-corridor as it angled toward Upper Level.

Somewhere around Middle Rivington, in a brush with three Newyorks, Alvah lost touch with Artie. He lost his man, too, in the warren of streets under the old Copter Terminal. When he came up for air, he found the streets full of terrified people—workmen, secretaries, whitecollars, porters, freewomen, all mixed up together like Knickerbocker Day and New Year's put together. They were packed so tight that many of them had climbed to the tops of abandoned floaters to escape the pressure. There was no room for them to move, but the nearest ones tried to make way for Alvah, just the same, when they saw his Muckfoot clothing.

He retreated, with a lump in his throat, and climbed to the nearest landing stage on the face of the building. Up and down the street, the stages were connected by stairs and railed walkways. No one was standing there, probably because of the green tendrils that spilled out of each stage entrance. Heads turned to watch him as he made his way northward. It was an up-and-down route, with a lot of stairs to climb and descend, but it was quicker and caused less anxiety than trying to move in the street.

He saw no blue-suited Newyorks, and no Muckfeet either, except for one man, glimpsed a block away as he crossed an intersection. Probably he ought to try underground again; but the airweed was getting so thick, he hated to do it. Mulling this over, he paused in Union Square to watch a curious procession emerging from the Mercy Hospital opposite.

A couple of Muckfeet in loose white jackets came first, then a dazed-looking nun; then a little group of men in hospital bathrobes, and then, towering over them all, a sinuous camel-colored animal with some sort of complex superstructure on its back. Moving on stilt-like legs, it picked its way delicately over a pileup of abandoned floaters at the edge of the walkway. After it, another one emerged from the hospital.

The confusing business on their backs, Alvah saw, was an arrangement of wickerwork baskets, each big enough for a man, suspended in gimbals so they swung level no matter how the beast moved. Each animal carried ten such baskets. Alvah recognized them now as the brutes Muckfeet called "ambulances." He had heard about them, but never seen one.

Three more burdened animals came out, then another group of walking patients, women this time, and with them three or four nuns, all with the same half startled, half bemused expression. Two Muckfoot women brought up the rear. As Alvah watched, one of the nuns stopped and began to tremble. One of the Muckfoot girls immediately stepped over and squeezed a bulb of something under her nose. Simultaneously, Alvah recognized the girl: it was Beej.

The nun's expression changed; she moved on dazedly and caught up with the rest of the group.

"Beej!" said Alvah, coming forward.

"Alvah!" They embraced.

"What is that stuff?" he asked. A fine mist hung around the nipple of the bulb she was still holding.

"Don't breathe any." Beej hurriedly capped the bulb and put it away. "It's a depressant, with a little tranquillizer mixed in—something to keep them calmed down for a while. These nuns is really wonderful, though, Alvah—they was scared to death, but they wouldn't leave their patients. We thought it be better not to separate them. Later on, after they get over the first shock, they can take care of them better than us.... My heaven, this place is *big* though, isn't it?"

"Yes," said Alvah with a sudden glumness.

She looked at him narrowly. "Don't feel bad, Alvah, it'll be better soon. You'll see."

"I know, but—"

They were passing the dark, green-hung doorway of an office building. Looking back over his shoulder, Alvah thought he caught a glimpse of movement deep in the shadowed interior. He paused.

"What's the matter?" asked Beej alertly.

A moving green figure bloomed. Alvah had just time to say, "Look out!" before the green curtains tore apart and a man came lurching down the ramp. He ran straight at Beej, brandishing a metal bar. He was a faceless man, smeared green from head to foot, making an inarticulate sound.

Alvah moved with what seemed painful slowness. He shouldered Beej aside as the bar came down, felt the blow numb his shoulder, and jabbed his knobkerrie at the other man's throat.

The man went down hard, arms and legs sprawled, and Alvah followed him with a two-handed swing that would have broken his head, if Alvah hadn't pulled back at the last moment. The sprawled figure was motionless. The metal bar tinkled on the pavement, somewhere to the left; it rolled, hit something and was silent.

Alvah prodded the man with his toe, then bent and worked open the hood closures. The face underneath was wide and muscular, with a stubborn strength in the jaw and brow. It was cyanosed, the lips blue-violet, the cheeks showing a bluish tinge under the skin. The eyes were rolled up behind half-open lids.

"Poor guy," said Alvah with sudden comprehension. "He was down in those corridors—the air conditioning's been off for hours." As he spoke, he was forcing open the chest zippers of the suit, unfastening the man's jacket and tunic underneath. He felt for a heartbeat, then straightened up slowly.

"He's dead," he said.

Beej went on with her charges; Alvah wandered back to the command post opposite the Armory, but the streets were full of terrified civilians, and the Muckfeet had gone elsewhere.

Alvah turned north again, and after half an hour or so ran into a Muckfoot detachment that was setting up a line of scarecrows on Second Avenue. The streets to westward were still full of people, crowding to get away. On the other side, the city looked deserted.

"We moving 'em along a block at a time," one of the Muckfeet told Alvah. "These here dummies—" he picked one up, a pole on a wooden base, with a gourd face and a cross-pole supporting the sleeves of an old Muckfoot jerkin—"scare 'em just as bad as we do. They started over by the wall, then moved back to here, and now we got them moving steady. Got to hunt through all that—" he waved at the deserted buildings behind him—"to make sure, but I guess we got most all of 'em out."

"What about the soldiers from the Armory?" Alvah asked.

"I saw some getting toted off," the Muckfoot said. "I b'lieve the boys took to slashing their suits with bowies, and then they didn't think they was invulnerable any more, so they quit."

An hour later, Knickerbocker Circle in Over Manhattan was littered with ameba-shaped puddles of clear plastic. Overhead, the stuff was hanging in festoons from the reticulated framework of the Roof and, for the first time in a century, an unfiltered wind was blowing into New York. Halfway up the sheer façade of the Old Movie House, a roc was flapping along, a wingtip almost brushing the louvers, while its rider sprinkled pale dust from a sack. Farther down the street, a sickly green growth was already visible on cornices and window frames.

The antique neon sign of the Old Movie dipped suddenly, its supports softened visibly. It swung, nodded and crashed to the pavement.

Alvah moved on. He had made contact with his squad again, finally, but nobody seemed to be urgently needing his help. The evacuation was going smoothly. The war was over. Alvah walked down the windy canyon of Upper Broadway, past Sammy's, where he had eaten cheesecake less than three weeks ago... it seemed like a century... past the silent Dramatic Arts Building and the empty realie palaces on Times Square, saying goodbye. Scuffed papers were littered along the walkway and in the freight channel. Grounded floaters were everywhere, empty, leaning against each other. The people were gone, and it began to seem wrong for Alvah to be there making echoes with his footsteps. He turned west again looking for company, feeling pretty low.

Twilight—all the streets that radiated from the heart of the City were afloat with long, slowly surging tides of humanity, dim in the weak glow from the lumen globes plastered haphazardly to the flanks of the buildings. At the end of every street, the Wall was crumbled down and the moat filled, its fire long gone out. And down the new railed walkways from all three levels came the men, women and children, stumbling out into the alien lumen-lit night and the strange scents and the wide world.

Watching from the hilltop, with his arm around his wife's waist, Alvah saw them being herded into groups and led away, unprotesting—saw them in the wains, rolling off toward the temporary shelters where, likely as not, they would sleep the night through, too numbed to be afraid of the morrow.

In the morning, their teaching would begin.

Babylon, Alvah thought, *Thebes, Angkor, Lagash, Agade, Tyre, Luxor, and now New York.*

A City grew out and then in—it was always the way, whether or not it had a Barrier around it. Growing, it crippled itself and its people—and died. The weeds overleaped its felled stones.

"Like an egg," B.J. said, although he had not spoken. *"Omne ex ovo* —but the eggshell has to break."

"I know," said Alvah, discovering that the empty ache in his belly was not sentiment but hunger. "Speaking of eggs—"

B.J. gave his arm a reassuring little pat. "Anything you want, dear. Radnip, orangoe, pearots, fleetmeat—*you* pick the menu."

Alvah's mouth began to water.

ABOUT THE AUTHOR

Damon Knight was an American science fiction author, editor, critic and fan. His forte was short stories and he is widely acknowledged as having been a master of the genre. He was a member of the Futurians, an early organization of the most prominent SF writers of the day. He founded the Science Fiction and Fantasy Writers of America, Inc. (SFWA), the primary writers' organization for genre writers, as well as the Milford Writers workshop and co-founded the Clarion Writers Workshop. He edited the notable Orbit anthology series, and received the Hugo and SFWA Grand Master award. The award was later renamed in his honor. He was married to fellow writer Kate Wilhelm.

More books from Damon Knight are available at:
www.ReAnimus.com/store/?author=Damon%20Knight

ReAnimus Press

CV, by Damon Knight
Info/buy:

The largest sea vessel ever built — and a deadly arena!

The Observers, by Damon Knight
Info/buy:

The alien plague returns, and CV is part of the sinister solution.

A Reasonable World, by Damon Knight
Info/buy:

CV #3... The symbionts are having a fascinating effect on people...

In Search of Wonder, by Damon Knight
Info/buy:

The premier book of SF insight for all SF readers and writers.

The World and Thorinn, by Damon Knight
Info/buy:

Thorinn is thrown into a well by his father to appease the rumbling gods... and down he goes!

Hell's Pavement, by Damon Knight
Info/buy:

There's a voice in your brain...but its not yours!

Beyond the Barrier, by Damon Knight
Info/buy:

Is the Professor human? Is he going to save Earth, or destory it?

A for Anything, by Damon Knight
Info/buy:

What if there was a machine that could duplicate anything?

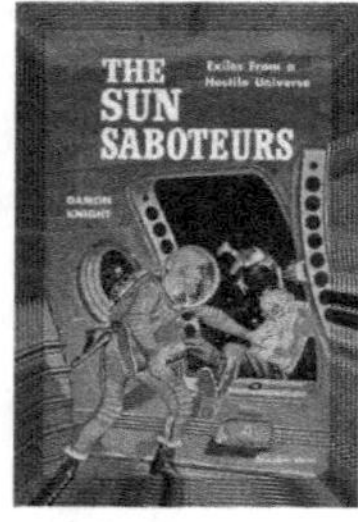

The Sun Saboteurs, by Damon Knight
Info/buy:

What happens if you fence off the humans?

The Rithian Terror, by Damon Knight
Info/buy:

A spy who can look like anyone threatens the Earth Empire

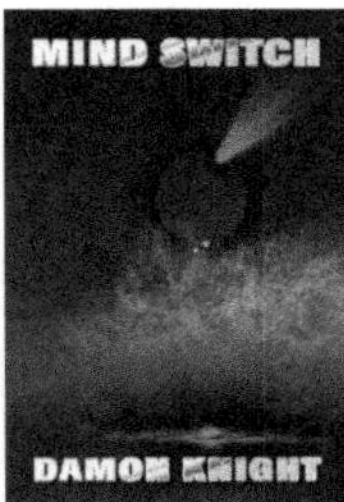

Mind Switch, by Damon Knight
Info/buy:

A visit to the zoo doesn't turn out as expected

The Man in the Tree, by Damon Knight
Info/buy:

Gene Anderson, poet, millionaire, circus freak--and can grab things from other universes

Why Do Birds, by Damon Knight
Info/buy:

Aliens send a man from the 1930s to build an ark to save humanity

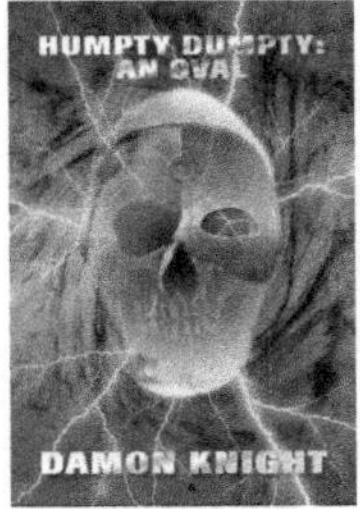

Humpty Dumpty: An Oval, by Damon Knight
Info/buy:

A bullet shatters reality... a surreal voyage and NYTimes Notable Book

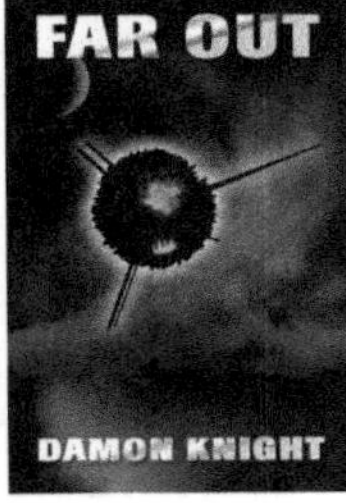

Far Out, by Damon Knight
Info/buy:

The Grandmaster's first collection of finest stories

In Deep, by Damon Knight
Info/buy:

An excellent collection of SFWA Grandmaster Damon Knight's stories

Off Center, by Damon Knight
Info/buy:

A collection of five short stories & novels from a SFWA Grandmaster

Turning On, by Damon Knight
Info/buy:

Another excellent collection of SFWA Grandmaster Damon Knight's stories

Three Novels, by Damon Knight
Info/buy:

World Without Children and The Earth Quarter, by Damon Knight
Info/buy:

Two fine novellas from the master.

 **Rule Golden and Other Stories,** by Damon Knight

Info/buy:

Five excellent short novels from a SFWA Grandmaster

Better Than One, by Damon Knight

Info/buy:

Late Knight Edition, by Damon Knight

Info/buy:

God's Nose, by Damon Knight

Info/buy:

One Side Laughing: Stories Unlike Other Stories, by Damon Knight

Info/buy:

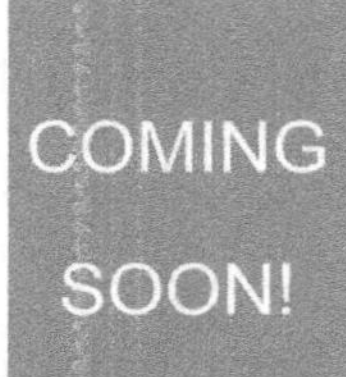

Turning Points: Essays on the Art of Science Fiction, by Damon Knight

Info/buy:

1939 Yearbook of Science, Weird and Fantasy Fiction, by Damon Knight

Info/buy:

Charles Fort, Prophet of the Unexplained, by Damon Knight

Info/buy:

Clarion Writers' Handbook, by Damon Knight

Info/buy:

Faking the Reader Out, by Damon Knight

Info/buy:

The Other Side of the Surface, by J. A. Lawrence

Info/buy:

Featuring the newly translated history concealed in SURFACE TENSION by James Blish

Sense of Wonder, by Gardner Dozois

Info/buy:

Gardner Dozois' collected reviews from Locus Magazine, amazing insights for any writer of SF fan.

Being Gardner Dozois, by Michael Swanwick

Info/buy:

Insights into the mind of the author/editor who holds the record for most Hugo awards for editing.

The Craft of Writing Science Fiction that Sells, by Ben Bova

Info/buy:

Learn how to write SF from the master! Ben Bova, best-selling author and six-time Hugo Award winner for Best Editor explains step by step all the elements you need to write professionally selling science fiction.

How To Improve Your Speculative Fiction Openings, by Robert Qualkinbush

Info/buy:

The secret that separates pro fiction from beginners', and how to capitalize on it.

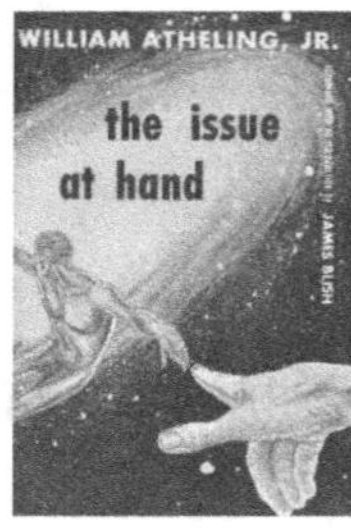
The Issue at Hand, by James Blish (as William Atheling, Jr.)

Info/buy:

No subject is taboo for Atheling's shredding, making this a textbook for authors and a delight for readers.

More Issues at Hand, by James Blish (as William Atheling, Jr.)

Info/buy:

More scalpel-sharp delights for the writer and reader.

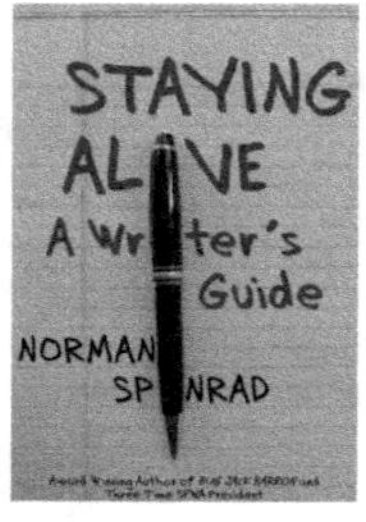
Staying Alive - A Writer's Guide, by Norman Spinrad

Info/buy:

How things really work in the art and commerce of publishing by a three-time SFWA President.

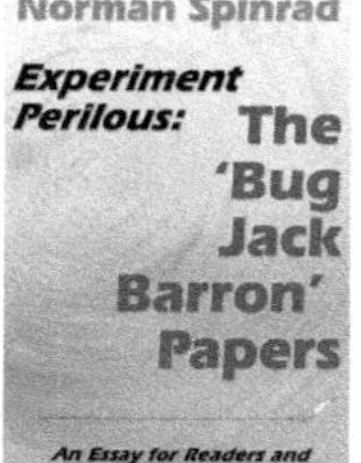
Experiment Perilous: The 'Bug Jack Barron' Papers, by Norman Spinrad

Info/buy:

A must-read essay for all Readers and Writers of Science Fiction

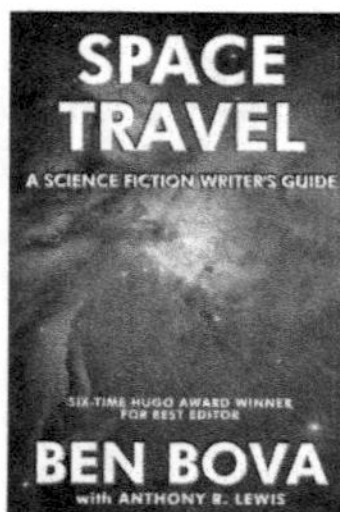
Space Travel - A Science Fiction Writer's Guide, by Ben Bova

Info/buy:

An indispensible tool for all science fiction writers, Space Travel explains the science you need to help you make your fiction plausible.

Anthopology 101: Reflections, Inspections and Dissections of SF Anthologies, by Bud Webster

Info/buy:

Bud expertly dissects the great SF anthologies. A must for writers and SF fans.

Past Masters, by Bud Webster

Info/buy:

A collection of some of Bud Webster's best SFnal columns

Having Relationships With Characters on the Road to Great Fiction, by Andrew Burt

Info/buy:

(Shhh! A Secret of Great Writing)

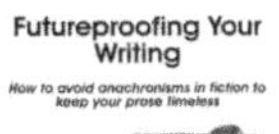

Futureproofing Your Writing, by Andrew Burt

Info/buy:

How to avoid anachronisms in fiction to keep your prose timeless.

Magic of Wild Places, by Bruce Taylor

Info/buy:

An author's struggles to understand his father, and his own power as a writer.

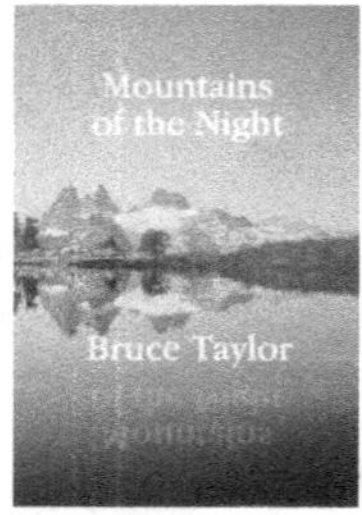

Mountains of the Night, by Bruce Taylor

Info/buy:

A writer's hike through a landscape of illness and family dysfunction to find for-giveness, courage and joy.

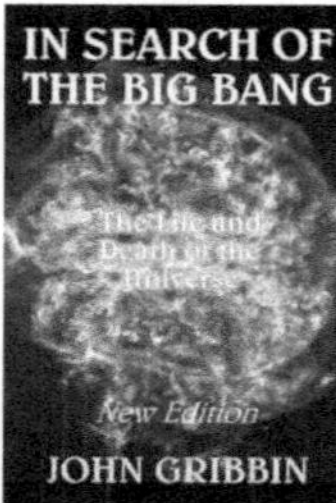

In Search of the Big Bang, by John Gribbin

Info/buy:

For Big Bang Theory fans, don't miss this indispensable guide! :) `A remarkably readable guide to the mysteries of cosmic creation' —Nature

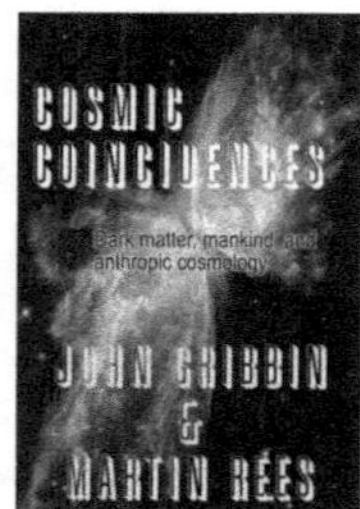

Cosmic Coincidences, by John Gribbin and Martin Rees

Info/buy:

A provocative search through space and time for a cosmic blueprint—and the source of life in the universe.

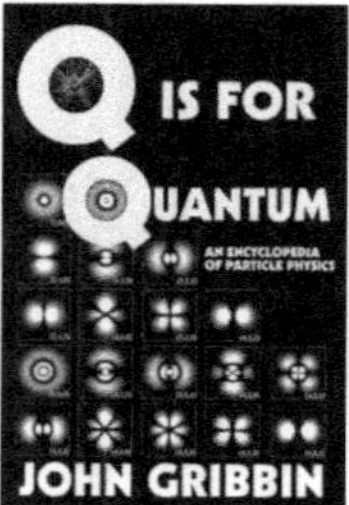

Q is for Quantum, by John Gribbin

Info/buy:

A comprehensive encyclopedia of quantum physics.

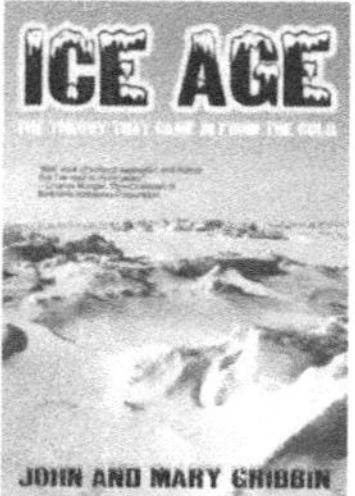

Ice Age, by John and Mary Gribbin

Info/buy:

The theory that came in from the cold...

In Search of the Double Helix, by John Gribbin

Info/buy:

Unraveling the mystery of life on earth...

Walls and Wonders, by S. R. Algernon

Info/buy:

Hugo finalist... If Hemingway wrote P.K.Dick-ian science fiction short stories...

Dreams of the Technarion, by Sean McMullen

Info/buy:

Stories from a Hugo finalist where the science might not be fiction! Plus the historical OUTPOST OF WONDER.

The Exiles Trilogy, by Ben Bova

Info/buy:

When all the best of Earth's scientists are exiled to a space station, they decide to embark on an even grander adventure to the stars. An epic trilogy in one volume.

The Star Conquerors (Collectors' Edition), by Ben Bova

Info/buy:

Special Collectors' Edition! Six time Hugo winner Ben Bova's most sought-after novel is now an ebook with the original Mel Hunter cover and an essay from Ben on the history of the book!

Colony, by Ben Bova
Info/buy:

Island One is a celestial utopia, and David Adams is its most perfect creation. But David is a prisoner, destined to spend his life in an island-sized cylinder orbiting a doomed home planet. David has a plan—one that will ultimately save humanity... or destroy it.

The Kinsman Saga, by Ben Bova
Info/buy:

Chet Kinsman is an astronaut ace who has done everything in space—including committing the first murder. Kinsman has to confront his hidden past and decide Earth's destiny, in a desperate countdown to nuclear annihilation.

Star Watchmen, by Ben Bova
Info/buy:

Mankind rules a giant galactic empire, but not all the worlds are pleased. Can the Star Watch prevent a revolt?

As on a Darkling Plain, by Ben Bova
Info/buy:

Dr. Sidney Lee races against time to prevent the huge alien machines on Titan from destroying mankind.

The Winds of Altair, by Ben Bova
Info/buy:

Altair VI isn't making it easy to Terraform!

Test of Fire, by Ben Bova
Info/buy:

A small group of survivors fight to rebuild civilization after the Earth is devastated by a huge solar flare.

The Weathermakers, by Ben Bova
Info/buy:

After conquering everything else, the last frontier was... controlling Mother Nature! By the award-winning hard SF author of the Grand Tour series.

The Dueling Machine, by Ben Bova
Info/buy:

Civilized, harmless virtual reality dueling has replaced all physical conflict — everything from punching someone over a personal insult to interstellar warfare... until a madman dictator of a small empire finds a way to cheat, and use the dueling machine to take over the galaxy!

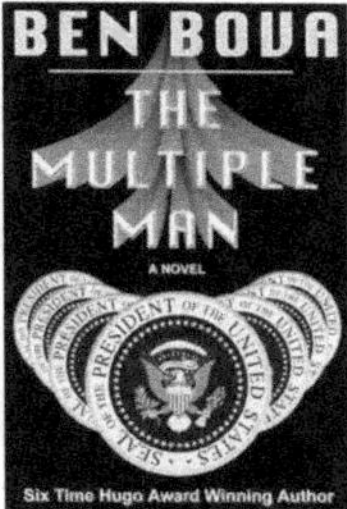 

The Multiple Man, by Ben Bova
Info/buy:

As the President is speaking inside an auditorium in Boston, the President's Press Secretary discovers a body in an alley outside: The body of the President.

Escape!, by Ben Bova
Info/buy:

No end to Danny's sentence, watched by a sentient computer, and no way out of the escape-proof prison, there was only one thing to do...

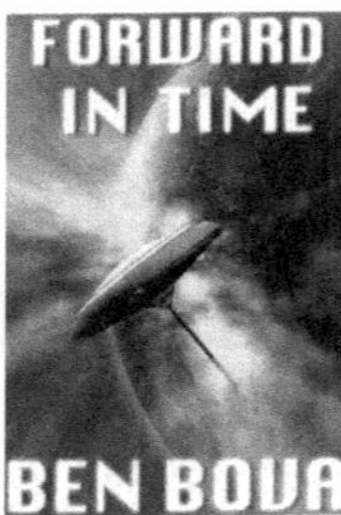

Forward in Time, by Ben Bova
Info/buy:

Get ready for a series of future shocks from the award-winning Ben Bova!

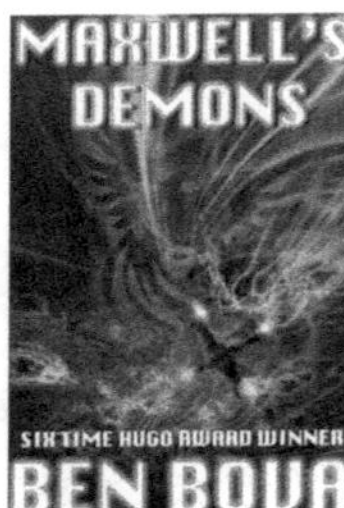

Maxwell's Demons, by Ben Bova
Info/buy:

Science fiction and science fact, humor and adventure, all await when you enter the unpredictable world of... MAXWELL'S DEMONS

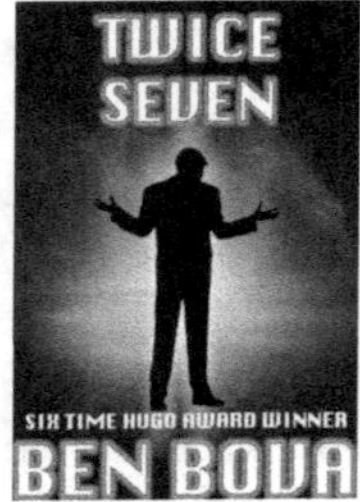

Twice Seven, by Ben Bova
Info/buy:

Ben Bova's universe is always more than the sum of its parts...

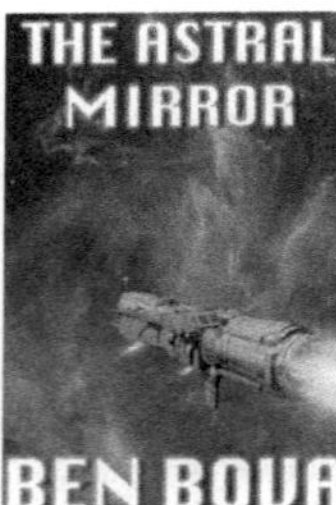

The Astral Mirror, by Ben Bova
Info/buy:

Here are a dozen and a half views of the world, past present and future, as seen through the Astral Mirror....

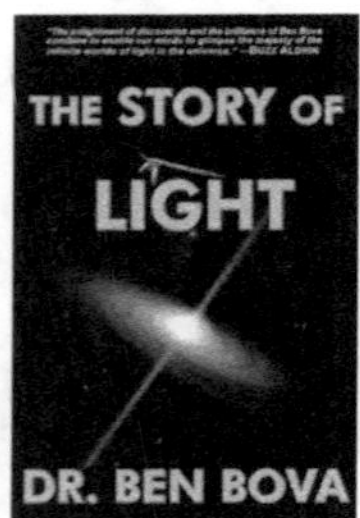

The Story of Light, by Ben Bova
Info/buy:

In this all-encompassing work, Ben Bova explores the subject of light and shows how it has shaped every aspect of our existence.

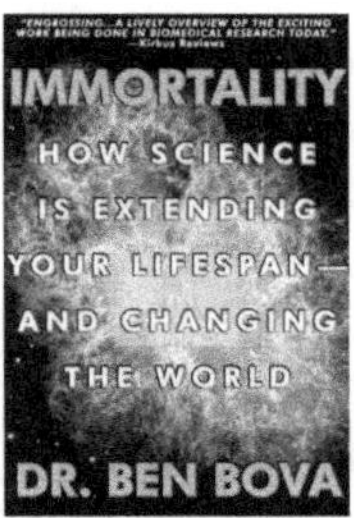

Immortality, by Ben Bova

Info/buy:

Dr. Bova explores the future effects of science and technology on the human life span. Death will no longer be the inevitable end of life.

Phoenix Without Ashes, by Harlan Ellison and Edward Bryant

Info/buy:

Co-written with Harlan Ellison and based on the award-winning script, the story of mankind's last salvation gone awry.

Shadrach in the Furnace, by Robert Silverberg

Info/buy:

Meet the new Khan! Soon to be immortal... A Hugo and Nebula Award Finalist novel from a Grand Master of science fiction.

Bloom, by Wil McCarthy

Info/buy:

In 2106, microscopic machine/creatures escape their creators to populate the inner solar system with a wild, deadly ecology all their own, pushing the tattered remnants of humanity out into the cold and dark of the outer planets. Seven astronauts must embark on mankind's boldest venture yet—the perilous journey home to infected Earth!

Aggressor Six, by Wil McCarthy

Info/buy:

An alien armada from the center of Orion makes its deadly way through the galaxy, destroying all human life in the process, and only Marine Corporal Kenneth Jonson and the Aggressor Six team can stop the onslaught.

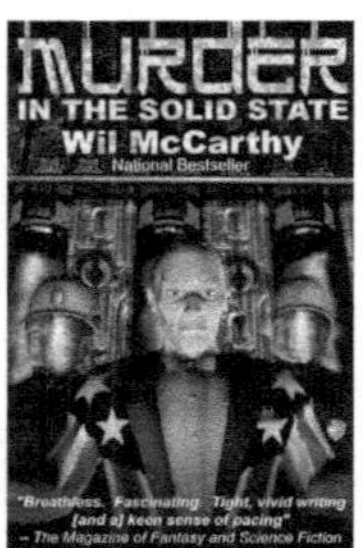

Murder in the Solid State, by Wil McCarthy

Info/buy:

David Sanger, an ambitious young physicist, attends a party at which a pompous older scientist, who just happens to have thwarted the younger man's innovative ideas, is murdered. Suddenly it is not just David's career, but his life that is at stake. Are his ideas that important? Who's out to stop David from changing the world?

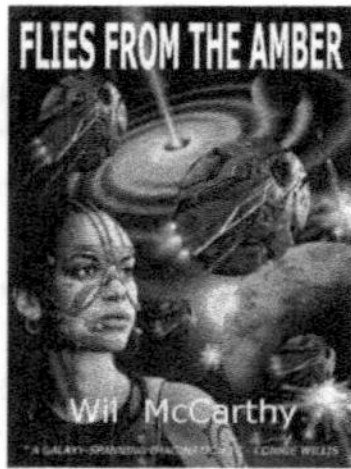

Flies from the Amber, by Wil McCarthy

Info/buy:

Forty light years from earth, the colonists on the world of Unua have somehow managed to keep civilization struggling on, despite twice daily earthquakes...

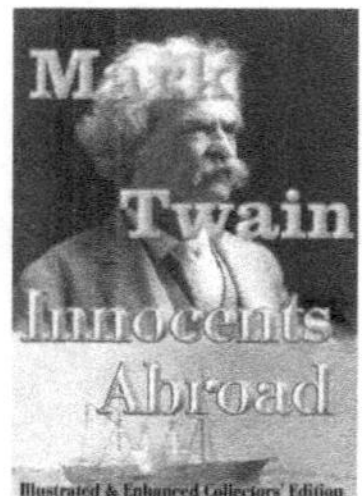

Innocents Abroad (Fully Illustrated & Enhanced Collectors' Edition), by Mark Twain

Info/buy:

Best. Travel. Book. Ever. (With all original illustrations.) Hilarious book about the first cruise from the US, visiting the Med.

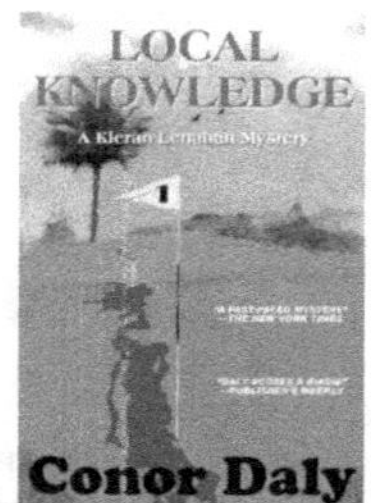

Local Knowledge (A Kieran Lenahan Mystery), by Conor Daly

Info/buy:

Lawyer-turned-golf pro Kieran Lenahan must solve the murder of millionaire country-club owner Sylvester Miles. "A FAST-PACED MYSTERY"—THE NEW YORK TIMES

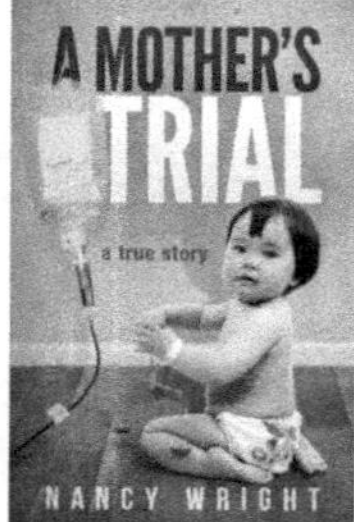

A Mother's Trial, by Nancy Wright

Info/buy:

Was it the perfect murder? A true story.

Bad Karma: A True Story of Obsession and Murder, by Deborah Blum

Info/buy:

The true story of a famous Berkeley murder and a landmark Supreme Court case.

Ghosts of Engines Past, by Sean McMullen

Info/buy:

Award winning steampunk from a master!

Colours of the Soul, by Sean McMullen

Info/buy:

Why are cheetahs the most perfect of creatures? Besides because they're cats, that is... Cool, mind-blowing stories from a master.

The Cure for Everything, by Severna Park

Info/buy:

Finding the cure for all diseases comes with a heavy price. Nebula Award winner!

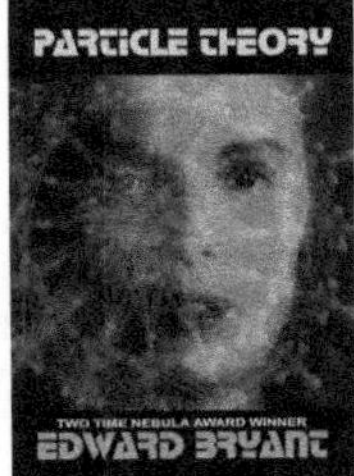

Particle Theory, by Edward Bryant

Info/buy:

Particle Theory by Edward Bryant : A collection of many of Ed's best works, including two Nebula Award winning short stories.

Commencement, by Roby James

Info/buy:

The Sting was what made Ronica McBride special—now she was crashed on an unknown planet without it.

Bug Jack Barron, by Norman Spinrad

Info/buy:

GET SET FOR THE BEST THING THAT EVER HAPPENED TO YOU! The banned book is back! You've heard of it, now you can read it! Lover and hero, Jack Barron, troubleshooter and media god of the Bug Jack Barron Show, has one last chance to hit it big when he meets Benedict Howards, the power-mad man with the secret to immortality. A Hugo and Nebula Award finalist!

The Last Hurrah of the Golden Horde, by Norman Spinrad

Info/buy:

"One of the greatest collections of science fiction short stories ever" — Goodreads.com

The Children of Hamelin, by Norman Spinrad

Info/buy:

A novel about the fast-lane life in the publishing world, by the award-winning Norman Spinrad.

One Against Herculum, by Jerry Sohl

Info/buy:

One of the famous Ace Doubles, with the wonderful original cover, One Against Herculum remains a fast-paced, fun story that you'll really enjoy.

Costigan s Needle, by Jerry Sohl

Info/buy:

What really was Dr. Costigan's tool for medical research? Where did the eye of the needle actually lead to?

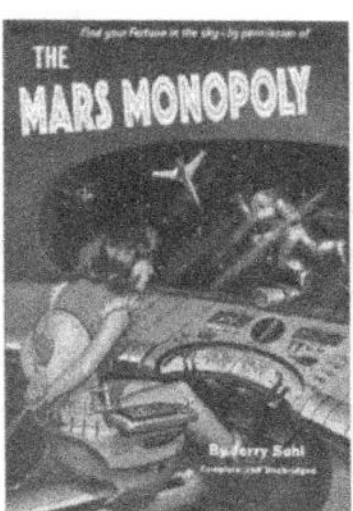

The Mars Monopoly, by Jerry Sohl

Info/buy:

One of the famous Ace Doubles, with the wonderful original cover, The Mars Monopoly still stands today as a great, fun story in the classic style.

The Sigil Trilogy (Omnibus vol.1-3), by Henry Gee

Info/buy:

The amazing Sigil Trilogy complete in one volume!

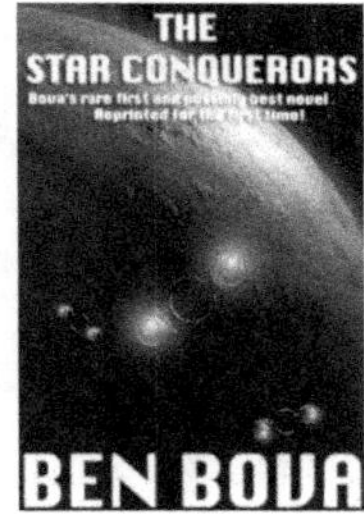

The Star Conquerors (Standard Edition), by Ben Bova

Info/buy:

Six time Hugo winner Ben Bova's most sought-after novel is back in print!

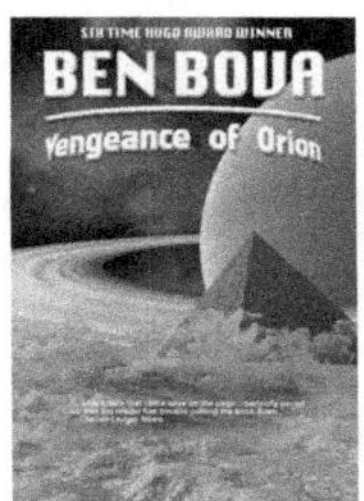

Vengeance of Orion, by Ben Bova

Info/buy:

Orion must travel back in time to change history and save Troy from the Greek army, or lose the only woman he has ever loved.

Orion in the Dying Time, by Ben Bova

Info/buy:

Time-traveling into the era of the dinosaurs, Orion must save the very fabric of spacetime from the satanic reptilian leader of the saurians.

Orion and the Conqueror, by Ben Bova

Info/buy:

Orion travels to the time of Alexander the Great, battling to save the future of mankind, and his own soul.

Orion Among the Stars, by Ben Bova

Info/buy:

The superhuman, time-traveling Orion leads interstellar warriors in a galactic war among the gods themselves.

The Starcrossed, by Ben Bova

Info/buy:

A stinging SFnal, futuristic satire on the TV industry, based a bit on reality.

To Save The Sun, by Ben Bova and A. J. Austin

Info/buy:

Earth's sun will soon explode, unless a massive engineering effort can save it.

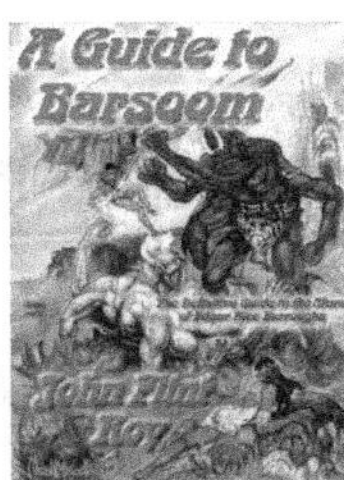

A Guide to Barsoom, by John Flint Roy

Info/buy:

THE OFFICIAL, DEFINITIVE GUIDE TO EDGAR RICE BURROUGH'S BAR-SOOM. Everything there is to know about John Carter of Mars and his world — the people, places and things, with maps and fully illustrated.

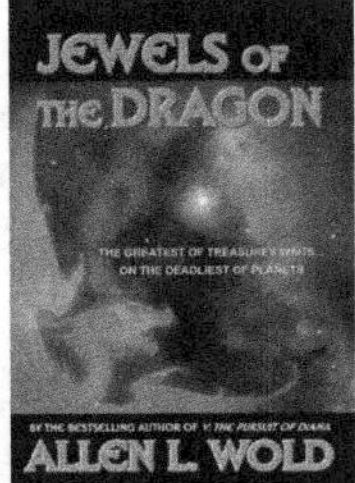

Jewels of the Dragon, by Allen L. Wold

Info/buy:

The greatest of treasures awaits... on the deadliest of planets.

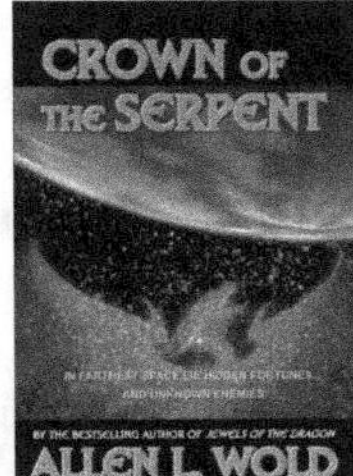

Crown of the Serpent, by Allen L. Wold

Info/buy:

In farthest space lie hidden fortunes... and unknown enemies.

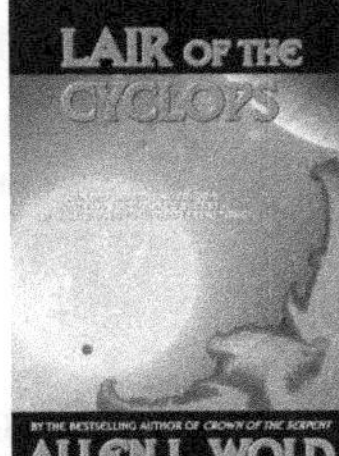

Lair of the Cyclops, by Allen L. Wold

Info/buy:

Rickard Braeth and friends must find the galaxy's secret—before it's used to destroy everything!

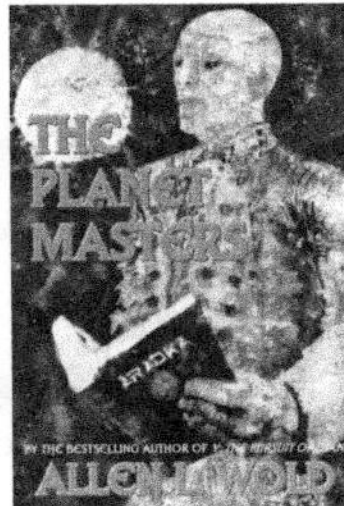

The Planet Masters, by Allen L. Wold

Info/buy:

Troubleshooter Larson McCade searches for the alien Book of Aradka on the planet Seltique, and may find more than he bargained for.

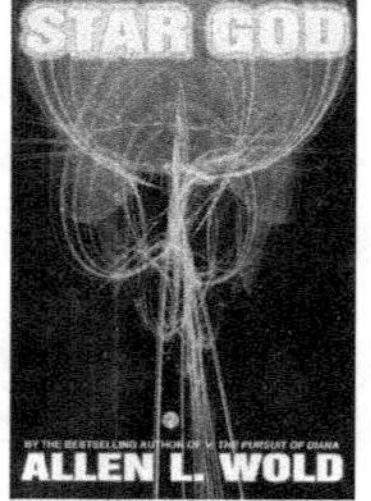

Star God, by Allen L. Wold

Info/buy:

There is a strange force at work in the universe. It must be stopped. But first, it must be understood.

Woman Without a Shadow, by Karen Haber

Info/buy:

War Minstrels #1. Kayla, an extraordinarily gifted young telepath, is on the run after challenging the most powerful families on her home planet, who've tried to take everything from her.

The War Minstrels, by Karen Haber

Info/buy:

War Minstrels #2. With powerful forces trying to stop the Free Traders, the starship Falstaff is no longer a safe refuge for renegade empath Kayla John Reed. Now her survival and all the War Minstrels' hinges upon her finding a legendary weapon.

Sister Blood, by Karen Haber

Info/buy:

War Minstrels #3. Empath Kayla and her War Minstrels must rescue her friends from the evil Yates, and prevent the destruction of all they've fought for.

The Sweet Taste of Regret, by Karen Haber

Info/buy:

Live anywhere you want... in any time... A collection of Karen Haber's best short fiction.

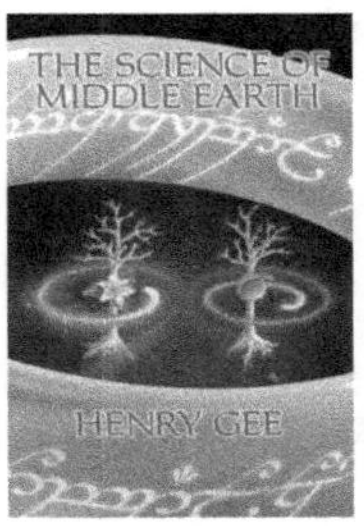

The Science of Middle-earth, by Henry Gee

Info/buy:

How did Frodo's mithril coat ward off the fatal blow of an orc? Can Balrogs fly? Nature editor Dr. Henry Gee explains how. A must-read for Tolkien fans.

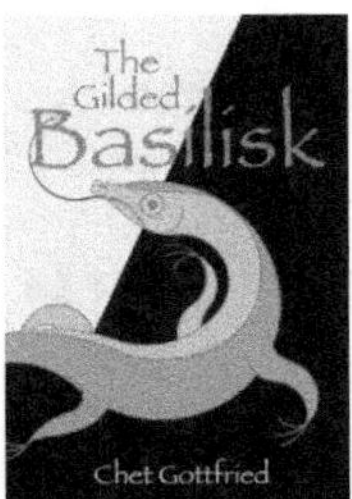

The Gilded Basilisk, by Chet Gottfried

Info/buy:

Add a basilisk, a dragon, and weirdragons to the mix-up of a theft going from bad to worse: Friends become enemies and enemies friends, wars loom, and the intrigues threaten the fate of two kingdoms.

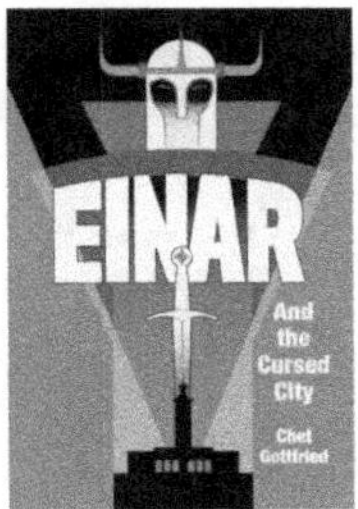

Einar and the Cursed City, by Chet Gottfried

Info/buy:

Sixteen-year-old Einar enters Jorghaven for dueling and desserts, but a curse has changed everyone except Barbara Bloodbath, who needs his help to free the city!

Neon Twilight, by Edward Bryant

Info/buy:

Neon Twilight by Edward Bryant : Three wonderful space opera stories, including Ed's Berserker story!

Trilobyte, by Edward Bryant

Info/buy:

A trio of twisted little tales from the master of twistedness.

Cinnabar, by Edward Bryant
Info/buy:

In the city at the center of time, paradox is just another urban renewal project.

Predators and Other Stories, by Edward Bryant
Info/buy:

Troubling tales as only Ed Bryant can tell. Don't miss the author introductions!

The Void Captain's Tale, by Norman Spinrad
Info/buy:

Symbiotically linked to her ship, Void Pilot Dominique Alia Wu senses something transcendent in the void...

The Time Dissolver, by Jerry Sohl
Info/buy:

How could they lose 11 years of their life—at the same time!? By a master of episodes from The Twilight Zone and Star Trek.

The Altered Ego, by Jerry Sohl
Info/buy:

Why would anyone murder a man marked for full body and brain restoration?

The Anomaly, by Jerry Sohl

Info/buy:

She couldn't have a baby... Then she got pregnant—but with what? By a master of episodes from The Twilight Zone and Star Trek.

The Haploids, by Jerry Sohl

Info/buy:

What is a Haploid? Are YOU a Haploid? A new take on an age-old battle! By a master of episodes from The Twilight Zone and Star Trek.

Underhanded Chess, by Jerry Sohl

Info/buy:

A hilarious handbook of devious diversions and stratagems for winning at chess.

Underhanded Bridge, by Jerry Sohl

Info/buy:

A hilarious handbook of devious diversions and stratagems for winning at bridge.

The Box: An Oral History of Television, 1920-1961, by Jeff Kisseloff

Info/buy:

"Wondrous... An oral scrapbook of the pioneering days of our video nation"—The New York Times Book Review

You Must Remember This: An Oral History of Manhattan from the 1890s to World War II, by Jeff Kisseloff

Info/buy:

Amazing stories of Manhattan from those who lived them.

Biff America: Steep Deep & Dyslexic, by Jeffrey Bergeron (AKA Biff America)

Info/buy:

A wonderfully funny mix of Andy Rooney and Garrison Keillor. Biff America poignantly writes what the American people need to know. Through it all, Biff America has a gift for revealing the uplifting realities of modern life and, sometimes, his humor will make you blow beer through your nose.

Side Effects, by Harvey Jacobs

Info/buy:

Vonnegut meets Catch-22! In the last hours of his hectic life, Simon Apple faces up to the hard truth that his very survival represents a prescription for disaster, not only for the pharmaceutical industry but for the nation itself! From award-winning author Harvey Jacobs.

American Goliath, by Harvey Jacobs

Info/buy:

The (mostly!) true story of America's greatest hoax, with a fantastic(al) twist from an award-winning author. [World Fantasy Award finalist!] "An inspired novel."—TIME Magazine. "A masterpiece...arguably this year's best novel."—Kirkus Reviews.

By The Sea, by Henry Gee

Info/buy:

A gothic modern scientific fiction horror mystery...